Mayne Reid

Gwen Wynn

Vol. 1

Mayne Reid

Gwen Wynn
Vol. 1

ISBN/EAN: 9783337346881

Printed in Europe, USA, Canada, Australia, Japan

Cover: Foto ©Andreas Hilbeck / pixelio.de

More available books at **www.hansebooks.com**

GWEN WYNN:

A Romance of the Wye.

BY

CAPTAIN MAYNE REID,

AUTHOR OF "LOST LENORE," "THE WHITE GAUNTLET," "HALF-BLOOD,"
"THE RIFLE RANGERS," "THE MAROON," ETC.

IN THREE VOLUMES.

VOL I.

LONDON:
TINSLEY BROTHERS, 8, CATHERINE STREET, STRAND.
1877.

LONDON:

PRINTED BY WOODFALL AND KINDER,

MILFORD LANE, STRAND, W.C.

CONTENTS.

GWEN WYNN:

A Romance of the Wye.

———

PROLOGUE.

HAIL to thee, Wye—famed river of Siluria!
Well deserving fame, worthy of warmest
salutation! From thy fountain-head on
Plinlimmon's far slope, where thou leapest
forth, gay as a girl on her skip-rope, through
the rugged rocks of Brecon and Radnor,
that like rude men would detain thee,
snatching but a kiss for their pains—on, as
woman grown, with statelier step, amid the
wooded hills of Herefordshire, which treat
thee with more courtly consideration—still
on, and once more rudely assailed by the
bold ramparts of Monmouth—through all
thou makest way—in despite all, preserving

thy purity! If defiled before espousing the ocean, the fault is not thine, but Sabrina's —sister born of thy birth, she too cradled on Plinlimmon's breast, but since childhood's days separated from thee, and straying through other shrines—perchance leading a less reputable life. No blame to thee, beautiful Vaga—from source to Severn pure as the spring that begets thee—fair to the eye, and full of interest to reflect on. Scarce a reach of thy channel, or curve of thy course, but is redolent of romance and rich in the lore of history. On thy shores, through the long centuries, has been enacted many a scene of gayest pleasure and sternest strife; many an exciting episode, in which love and hate, avarice and ambition—in short, every human passion has had play. Overjoyed were the Roman Legionaries to behold their silver eagles reflected from thy pellucid wave; though they did not succeed in planting them on thy western shore till after many a tough struggle with the gallant, but ill-starred, Caractacus. Long, too, had the Saxons to battle before they

could make good their footing on the
Silurian side—as witness the Dyke of Offa.
Later, the Normans obtained it only through
treachery, by the murder of the princely
Llewellyn; and, later still, did the bold
Glendower make thy banks the scene of
patriotic strife; while, last of all, sawest
thou conflict in still nobler cause—as of
more glorious remembrance — when the
earnest soldiers. of the Parliament encoun-
tered the so-called Cavaliers, and purged
thy shores of the ribald rout, making them
pure as thy waters.

But, sweet Wye! not all the scenes thou
hast witnessed have been of war. Love,
too, has stamped thee with many a tender
souvenir, many a tale of warm wild passion.
Was it not upon thy banks that the handsome "Harry of Monmouth," hero of
Agincourt, first saw the light; there living,
till manhood-grown, when he appeared
"armed *cap-à-pie*, with beaver on"? And
did not thy limpid waters bathe the feet of
Fair Rosamond, in childhood's days, when
she herself was pure? In thee, also, was

mirrored the comely form of Owen Tudor, which caught the eye of a queen—the stately Catharine—giving to England a race of kings; and by thy side the beauteous Saxon, Ædgitha, bestowed her heart and hand on a Cymric prince.

Nor are such episodes all of the remote past, but passing now; now, as ever, pathetic—as ever impassioned. For still upon thy banks, Vaga, are men brave, and women fair, as when Adelgisa excited the jealousy of the Druid priestess, or the maid of Clifford Castle captured a king's heart, to become the victim of a queen's vengeance.

Not any fairer than the heroine of my tale; and she was born there, there brought up, and there——

Ah! that is the story to be told.

CHAPTER I.

A TOURIST descending the Wye by boat from the town of Hereford to the ruined Abbey of Tintern, may observe on its banks a small pagoda-like structure; its roof, with a portion of the supporting columns, o'er-topping a spray of evergreens. It is simply a summer-house, of the kiosk or pavilion pattern, standing in the ornamental grounds of a gentleman's residence. Though placed conspicuously on an elevated point, the boat traveller obtains view of it only from a reach of the river above. When opposite he loses sight of it; a spinny of tall poplars drawing curtain-like between him and the higher bank. These stand on an oblong island, which extends several hundred yards down the stream, formed by an old channel, now forsaken. With all its wanderings the Wye is not suddenly capricious; still, in the lapse of long ages it has here and there changed its course, forming *aits*, or *eyots*, of which this is one.

The tourist will not likely take the abandoned channel. He is bound and booked for Tintern—possibly Chepstow—and will not be delayed by lesser "lions." Besides, his hired boatmen would not deviate from their terms of charter, without adding an extra to their fare.

Were he free, and disposed for exploration, entering this unused water way, he would find it tortuous, with scarce any current, save in times of flood; on one side the eyot, a low marshy flat, thickly overgrown with trees; on the other a continuous cliff, rising forty feet sheer, its *façade* grim and grey, with flakes of reddish hue, where the frost has detached pieces from the rock —the old red sandstone of Herefordshire. Near its entrance he would catch a glimpse of the kiosk on its crest; and, proceeding onward, will observe the tops of laurels and other exotic evergreens, mingling their glabrous foliage with that of the indigenous holly, ivy, and ferns; these last trailing over the cliff's brow, and wreathing it with fillets of verdure, as if to conceal its frowning corrugations.

About midway down the old river's bed he will arrive opposite a little embayment in the high bank, partly natural, but in part quarried out of the cliff—as evinced by a flight of steps, leading up at back, chiselled out of the rock *in situ*.

The cove thus contrived is just large enough to give room to a row-boat; and, if not out upon the river, one will be in it, riding upon its painter; this attached to a ring in the red sandstone. It is a light two-oared affair—a pleasure-boat, ornamentally painted, with cushioned thwarts, and tiller ropes of coloured cord athwart its stern, which the tourist will have turned towards him, in gold lettering, " THE GWENDOLINE."

Charmed by this Idyllic picture, he may forsake his own craft, and ascend to the top of the stair. If so, he will have before his eyes a lawn of park-like expanse, mottled with clumps of coppice, here and there a grand old tree—oak, elm, or chestnut— standing solitary; at the upper end a shrubbery of glistening evergreens, with gravelled walks, fronting a handsome house; or, in the parlance of the estate agent, a noble mansion. That is Llangorren Court, and there dwells the owner of the pleasure-boat, as also prospective owner of the house, with some two thousand acres of land lying adjacent.

The boat bears her baptismal name, the surname being Wynn, while people, in a familiar way, speak of her as "Gwen Wynn;" this on account of her being a lady of proclivities and habits that make her somewhat of a celebrity in the neigh-bourhood. She not only goes boating, but hunts, drives a pair of spirited horses, pre-sides over the church choir, plays its organ, looks after the poor of the parish—nearly all of it her own, or soon to be—and has a bright smile, with a pleasant word, for everybody.

If she be outside, upon the lawn, the tourist, supposing him a gentleman, will withdraw; for across the grounds of Llangorren Court there is no "right of way," and the presence of a stranger upon them would be deemed an intrusion. Nevertheless, he would go back down the boat-stair reluctantly, and with a sigh of regret, that good manners do not permit his making the acquaintance of Gwen Wynn without further loss of time, or any ceremony of introduction.

But my readers are not thus debarred; and to them I introduce her, as she saunters over this same lawn, on a lovely April morn.

She is not alone; another lady, by name Eleanor Lees, being with her. They are nearly of the same age—both turned twenty—but in all other respects unlike, even to contrast, though there is kinship between them. Gwendoline Wynn is tall of form, fully developed; face of radiant brightness, with blue-grey eyes, and hair of that chrome yellow almost peculiar to the

Cymri—said to have made such havoc with the hearts of the Roman soldiers, causing these to deplore the day when recalled home to protect their seven-hilled city from Goths and Visigoths.

In personal appearance Eleanor Lees is the reverse of all this; being of dark complexion, brown-haired, black-eyed, with a figure slender and *petite*. Withal she is pretty; but it is only prettiness—a word inapplicable to her kinswoman, who is pronouncedly beautiful.

Equally unlike are they in mental characteristics; the first-named being free of speech, courageous, just a trifle fast, and possibly a little imperious. The other of a reserved, timid disposition, and habitually of subdued mien, as befits her station; for in this there is also disparity between them —again a contrast. Both are orphans; but it is an orphanage under widely different circumstances and conditions: the one heiress to an estate worth some ten thousand pounds per annum; the other inheriting nought save an old family name—indeed, left without other means of livelihood, than what she may derive from a superior education she has received.

Notwithstanding their inequality of fortune, and the very distant relationship—for they are not even near as cousins—the rich girl behaves towards the poor one as though they were sisters. No one seeing them stroll arm-in-arm through the shrubbery, and hearing them hold converse in familiar, affectionate tones, would suspect the little dark damsel to be the paid "companion" of the lady by her side. Yet in such capacity is she residing at Llangorren Court.

It is just after the hour of breakfast, and they have come forth in morning robes of light muslin—dresses suitable to the day and the season. Two handsome ponies are upon the lawn, its herbage dividing their attention with the horns of a pet stag, which now and then threaten to assail them.

All three, soon as perceiving the ladies, trot towards them; the ponies stretching out their necks to be patted; the cloven-hoofed creature equally courting caresses.

They look especially to Miss Wynn, who is more their mistress.

On this particular morning she does not seem in the humour for dallying with them ; nor has she brought out their usual allowance of lump sugar ; but, after a touch with her delicate fingers, and a kindly exclamation, passes on, leaving them behind, to all appearance disappointed.

"Where are you going, Gwen ?" asks the companion, seeing her step out straight, and apparently with thoughts preoccupied. Their arms are now disunited, the little incident with the animals having separated them.

"To the summer-house," is the response. "I wish to have a look at the river. It should show fine this bright morning."

And so it does; as both perceive after entering the pavilion, which commands a view of the valley, with a reach of the river above—the latter, under the sun, glistening like freshly polished silver.

Gwen views it through a glass—a binocular she has brought out with her; this

of itself proclaiming some purpose afore-
thought, but not confided to the companion.
It is only after she has been long holding it
steadily to her eye, that the latter fancies
there must be some object within its field
of view more interesting than the Wye's
water, or the greenery on its banks.

" What is it ? " she naïvely asks. " You
see something ? "

" Only a boat," answers Gwen, bringing
down the glass with a guilty look, as if
conscious of being caught. " Some tourist,
I suppose, making down to Tintern Abbey
—like as not, a London cockney."

The young lady is telling a " white lie."
She knows the occupant of that boat is
nothing of the kind. From London he
may be—she cannot tell—but certainly no
sprig of cockneydom—unlike it as Hyperion
to the Satyr; at least so she thinks. But
she does not give her thought to the companion ; instead, concealing it, she adds,—

" How fond those town people are of
touring it upon our Wye ! "

" Can you wonder at that ? " asks Ellen.

"Its scenery is so grand—I should say, incomparable; nothing equal to it in England."

"I don't wonder," says Miss Wynn, replying to the question. "I'm only a little bit vexed seeing them there. It's like the desecration of some sacred stream, leaving scraps of newspapers in which they wrap their sandwiches, with other picnicking débris on its banks! To say nought of one's having to encounter the rude fellows that in these degenerate days go a-rowing —shopboys from the towns, farm labourers, colliers, hauliers, all sorts. I've half a mind to set fire to the *Gwendoline*, burn her up, and never again lay hand on an oar."

Ellen Lees laughs incredulously as she makes rejoinder.

"It would be a pity," she says, in serio-comic tone. "Besides, the poor people are entitled to a little recreation. They don't have too much of it."

"Ah, true," rejoins Gwen, who, despite her grandeeism, is neither Tory nor aristo-

crat. "Well, I've not yet decided on that
little bit of incendiarism, and shan't burn
the *Gwendoline*—at all events not till we've
had another row out of her."

Not for a hundred pounds would she set
fire to that boat, and never in her life was
she less thinking of such a thing. For just
then she has other views regarding the
pretty pleasure craft, and intends taking
seat on its thwarts within less than twenty
minutes' time.

"By the way," she says, as if the thought
had suddenly occurred to her, "we may as
well have that row now—whether it's to be
the last or not."

Cunning creature! She has had it in
her mind all the morning; first from her
bed-chamber window, then from that of the
breakfast-room, looking up the river's reach,
with the binocular at her eye, too, to note
if a certain boat, with a salmon-rod bending over it, passes down. For one of its
occupants is an angler.

"The day's superb," she goes on; "sun's
not too hot—gentle breeze—just the weather

for a row.   And the river looks so inviting
—seems calling us to come!   What say
you, Nell?"

"Oh! I've no objections."

"Let us in, then, and make ready.   Be
quick about it!   Remember it's April, and
there may be showers.   We mustn't miss a
moment of that sweet sunshine."

At this the two forsake the summer-
house; and, lightly recrossing the lawn,
disappear within the dwelling.

  * * * * *

While the angler's boat is still opposite
the grounds, going on, eyes are observing it
from an upper window of the house; again
those of Miss Wynn herself, inside her
dressing-room, getting ready for the river.

She had only short glimpses of it, over
the tops of the trees on the eyot, and now
and then through breaks in their thinner
spray.   Enough, however, to assure her
that it contains two men, neither of them
cockneys.   One at the oars she takes to be
a professional waterman.   But he, seated
in the stern is altogether unknown to her,

save by sight—that obtained when twice
meeting him out on the river. She knows
not whence he comes, or where he is residing; but supposes him a stranger to the
neighbourhood, stopping at some hotel. If
at the house of any of the neighbouring
gentry, she would certainly have heard of
it. She is not even acquainted with his
name, though longing to learn it. But she
is shy to inquire, lest that might betray
her interest in him. For such she feels, has
felt, ever since setting eyes on his strangely
handsome face.

As the boat again disappears behind the
thick foliage, she sets, in haste, to effect the
proposed change of dress, saying, in soliloquy—for she is now alone :—

"I wonder who, and what he can be ? A
gentleman, of course. But, then, there are
gentlemen, and gentlemen; single ones
and——"

She has the word "married" on her
tongue, but refrains speaking it. Instead,
she gives utterance to a sigh, followed by
the reflection—

"Ah, me! That would be a pity—a dis——"

Again she checks herself, the thought being enough unpleasant without the words.

Standing before the mirror, and sticking long pins into her hair, to keep its rebellious plaits in their place, she continues soliloquising—

"If one only had a word with that young waterman who rows him! And were it not that my own boatman is such a chatterer, I'd put him up to getting that word. But no! It would never do. He'd tell aunt about it; and then Madame la Chatelaine would be talking all sorts of serious things to me—the which I mightn't relish. Well; in six months more the old lady's trusteeship of this young lady is to terminate—at least legally. Then I'll be my own mistress; and then—'twill be time enough to consider whether I ought to have—a master. Ha, ha, ha!"

So laughing, as she surveys her superb figure in a cheval glass, she completes the adjustment of her dress, by setting a hat upon her head, and tightening the elastic, to secure against its being blown off while in the boat. In fine, with a parting glance at the mirror, which shows a satisfied expression upon her features, she trips lightly out of the room, and on down the stairway.

CHAPTER II.

THE HERO.

THAN Vivian Ryecroft—handsomer man never carried sling-jacket over his shoulder, or sabretasche on his hip. For he is in the Hussars—a captain.

He is not on duty now, nor anywhere near the scene of it. His regiment is at Aldershot, himself rusticating in Hereford-shire—whither he has come to spend a few weeks' leave of absence.

Nor is he, at the time of our meeting him, in the saddle, which he sits so grace-fully; but in a row-boat on the river Wye —the same just sighted by Gwen Wynn through the double lens of her lorgnette. No more is he wearing the braided uniform and "busby;" but, instead, attired in a suit of light Cheviots, piscator-cut, with a helmet-shaped cap of quilted cotton on his

head, its rounded rim of spotless white in
striking, but becoming, contrast with his
bronzed complexion and dark military
moustache.

For Captain Ryecroft is no mere stripling
nor beardless youth, but a man turned
thirty, browned by exposure to Indian
suns, experienced in Indian campaigns,
from those of Scinde and the Punjaub to
that most memorable of all—the Mutiny.

Still is he personally as attractive as he
ever was—to women, possibly more; among
these causing a flutter, with *rapprochement*
towards him almost instinctive, when and
wherever they may meet him. In the
present many a bright English lady sighs
for him, as in the past many a dark damsel
of Hindostan. And without his heaving
sigh, or even giving them a thought in
return. Not that he is of cold nature, or
in any sense austere; instead, warm-hearted,
of cheerful disposition, and rather partial to
female society. But he is not, and never
has been, either man-flirt or frivolous trifler;
else he would not be fly-fishing on the Wye

—for that is what he is doing there— instead of in London, taking part in the festivities of the "season," by day dawdling in Rotten Row, by night exhibiting himself in opera-box or ball-room. In short, Vivian Ryecroft is one of those rare individuals, to a high degree endowed, physically as mentally, without being aware of it, or appearing so ; while to all others it is very perceptible.

He has been about a fortnight in the neighbourhood, stopping at the chief hotel of a riverine town much affected by fly-fishermen and tourists. Still, he has made no acquaintance with the resident gentry. He might, if wishing it ; which he does not, his purpose upon the Wye not being to seek society, but salmon, or rather the sport of taking it. An ardent disciple of the ancient Izaak, he cares for nought else— at least, in the district where he is for the present sojourning.

Such is his mental condition, up to a certain morning ; when a change comes over it, sudden as the spring of a salmon at

the gaudiest or most tempting of his flies
—this brought about by a face, of which he
has caught sight by merest accident, and
while following his favourite occupation.
Thus it has chanced :—

Below the town where he is staying, some
four or five miles by the course of the
stream, he has discovered one of those
places called " catches," where the king of
river fish delights to leap at flies, whether
natural or artificial—a sport it has oft
reason to rue. Several times so, at the
end of Captain Ryecroft's line and rod ;
he having there twice hooked a twenty-
pounder, and once a still larger specimen,
which turned the scale at thirty. In consequence that portion of the stream has
become his choicest angling ground, and at
least three days in the week he repairs to
it. The row is not much going down, but
a good deal returning ; five miles up stream,
most of it strong adverse current. That,
however, is less his affair than his oarsman's
—a young waterman by name Wingate,
whose boat and services the hussar officer

has chartered by the week—indeed, engaged them for so long as he may remain upon the Wye.

On the morning in question, dropping down the river to his accustomed whipping-place, but at a somewhat later hour than usual, he meets another boat coming up— a pleasure craft, as shown by its style of outside ornament and inside furniture. Of neither does the salmon fisher take much note; his eyes all occupied with those upon the thwarts. There are three of them, two being ladies seated in the stern sheets, the third an oarsman on a thwart well forward, to make better balance. And to the latter the hussar officer gives but a glance—just to observe that he is a serving-man—wearing some of its insignia in the shape of a cockaded hat, and striped stable-waistcoat. And not much more than a glance at one of the former; but a gaze, concentrated and long as good manners will permit, at the other, who is steering; when she passes beyond sight, her face remaining in his memory, vivid as if still before his eyes.

All this at a first encounter; repeated in a second, which occurs on the day succeeding, under similar circumstances, and almost in the self-same spot; then the face, if possible, seeming fairer, and the impression made by it on Vivian Ryecroft's mind sinking deeper—indeed, promising to be permanent. It is a radiant face, set in a luxuriance of bright amber hair—for it is that of Gwendoline Wynn.

On the second occasion he has a better view of her, the boats passing nearer to one another; still, not so near as he could wish, good manners again interfering. For all, he feels well satisfied—especially with the thought, that his own gaze earnestly given, though under such restraint, has been with earnestness returned. Would that his secret admiration of its owner were in like manner reciprocated !

Such is his reflective wish as the boats widen the distance between; one labouring slowly up, the other gliding swiftly down.

His boatman cannot tell who the lady is, nor where she lives. On the second day he

is not asked—the question having been put
to him on that preceding. All the added
knowledge now obtained is the name of the
craft that carries her; which, after passing,
the waterman, with face turned towards its
stern, makes out to be the *Gwendoline*—
just as on his own boat—the *Mary,*—
though not in such grand golden letters.

It may assist Captain Ryecroft in his
inquiries, already contemplated, and he
makes note of it.

Another night passes; another sun shines
over the Wye; and he again drops down
stream to his usual place of sport—this day
only to draw blank, neither catching salmon,
nor seeing hair of amber hue; his reflecting on which is, perchance, a cause of the
fish not taking to his flies, cast carelessly.

He is not discouraged; but goes again
on the day succeeding—that same when his
boat is viewed through the binocular. He
has already formed a half suspicion that
the home of the interesting water nymph
is not far from that pagoda-like structure,
he has frequently noticed on the right bank

of the river. For, just below the outlying eyot is where he has met the pleasure-boat, and the old oarsman looked anything but equal to a long pull up stream. Still, between that and the town are several other gentlemen's residences on the river side, with some standing inland. It may be any of them.

But it is not, as Captain Ryecroft now feels sure, at sight of some floating drapery in the pavilion, with two female heads showing over its baluster rail; one of them with tresses glistening in the sunlight, bright as sunbeams themselves.

He views it through a telescope—for he, too, has come out provided for distant observation—this confirming his conjectures just in the way he would wish. Now there will be no difficulty in learning who the lady is—for of one only does he care to make inquiry.

He would order Wingate to hold way, but does not relish the idea of letting the waterman into his secret; and so, remaining silent, he is soon carried beyond sight of the summer-house, and along the outer edge of the islet, with its curtain of tall trees coming invidiously between.

Continuing on to his angling ground, he gives way to reflections—at first of a pleasant nature. Satisfactory to think that she, the subject of them, at least lives in a handsome house; for a glimpse got of its upper storey tells it to be this. That she is in social rank a lady, he has hitherto had no doubt. The pretty pleasure craft and its appendages, with the venerable domestic acting as oarsman, are all proofs of something more than mere respectability—rather evidences of style.

Marring these agreeable considerations is the thought, he may not to-day meet the pleasure-boat. It is the hour that, from past experience, he might expect it to be out—for he has so timed his own piscatorial excursion. But, seeing the ladies in the summer-house, he doubts getting nearer sight of them—at least for another twenty-four hours. In all likelihood they have been already on the river, and returned home again. Why did he not start earlier?

While thus fretting himself, he catches sight of another boat—of a sort very different from the *Gwendoline*—a heavy barge-like affair, with four men in it; hulking fellows, to whom rowing is evidently a new experience. Notwithstanding this, they do not seem at all frightened at finding themselves upon the water. Instead, they are behaving in a way that shows them either very courageous, or very regardless of a danger—which, possibly, they are not aware of. At short intervals one or other is seen starting to his feet, and rushing fore or aft—as if on an empty coal-waggon, instead of in a boat—and in such fashion, that were the craft at all crank, it would certainly be upset!

On drawing nearer them Captain Rye-croft and his oarsman get the explanation of their seemingly eccentric behaviour—its cause made clear by a black bottle, which one of them is holding in his hand, each of the others brandishing tumbler, or teacup. They are drinking; and that they have been so occupied for some time is evident by their loud shouts, and grotesque gesturing.

"They look an ugly lot!" observes the young waterman, viewing them over his shoulder; for, seated at the oars, his back is towards them. "Coal fellows, from the Forest o' Dean, I take it."

Ryecroft, with a cigar between his teeth, dreamily thinking of a boat with people in it so dissimilar, simply signifies assent with a nod.

But soon he is roused from his reverie, at hearing an exclamation louder than common, followed by words whose import concerns himself and his companion. These are :—

"Dang it, lads! le's goo in for a bit o' a lark! Yonner be a boat coomin' down wi' two chaps in 't; some o' them spickspan city gents! S'pose we gie 'em a capsize?"

"Le's do it! Le's duck 'em!" shouted the others, assentingly; he with the bottle

dropping it into the boat's bottom, and laying hold of an oar instead.

All act likewise, for it is a four-oared craft
that carries them; and in a few seconds'
time they are rowing it straight for that of
the angler's.

With astonishment, and fast gathering
indignation, the Hussar officer sees the
heavy barge coming bow on for his light
fishing skiff, and is thoroughly sensible of
the danger; the waterman becoming aware
of it at the same instant of time.

"They mean mischief," mutters Wingate; "what'd we best do, Captain? If
you like I can keep clear, and shoot the
Mary past 'em—easy enough."

"Do so," returns the salmon fisher, with
the cigar still between his teeth—but now
held bitterly tight, almost to biting off the
stump. "You can keep on!" he adds,
speaking calmly, and with an effort to keep
down his temper; "that will be the best
way, as things stand now. They look like
they'd come up from below; and, if they
show any ill manners at meeting, we can

call them to account on return. Don't concern yourself about your course. I'll see to the steering. There! hard on the starboard oar!"

This last, as the two boats have arrived within less than three lengths of one another. At the same time Ryecroft, drawing tight the port tiller-cord, changes course suddenly, leaving just sufficient sea-way for his oarsman to shave past, and avoid the threatened collision.

Which is done the instant after—to the discomfiture of the would-be capsizers. As the skiff glides lightly beyond their reach, dancing over the river swell, as if in triumph and to mock them, they drop their oars, and send after it a chorus of yells, mingled with blasphemous imprecations.

In a lull between, the Hussar officer at length takes the cigar from his lips, and calls back to them—

"You ruffians! You shall rue it! Shout on—till you're hoarse. There's a reckoning for you, perhaps sooner than you expect."

"Yes, ye d—d scoun'rels!" adds the
young waterman, himself so enraged as
almost to foam at the mouth. "Ye'll have
to pay dear for sich a dastartly attemp' to
waylay Jack Wingate's boat. That will
ye."

"Bah!" jeeringly retorts one of the
roughs. "To blazes wi' you, an' yer boat!"

"Ay, to the blazes wi' ye!" echo the
others in drunken chorus; and, while their
voices are still reverberating along the adjacent cliffs, the fishing skiff drifts round a
bend of the river, bearing its owner and
his fare out of their sight, as beyond ear-
shot of their profane speech.

CHAPTER III.

THE lawn of Llangorren Court, for a time abandoned to the dumb quadrupeds, that had returned to their tranquil pasturing, is again enlivened by the presence of the two young ladies; but so transformed, that they are scarce recognisable as the same late seen upon it. Of course, it is their dresses that have caused the change; Miss Wynn now wearing a pea jacket of navy blue, with anchor buttons, and a straw hat set coquettishly on her head, its ribbons of azure hue trailing over, and prettily contrasting with the plaits of her chrome-yellow hair, gathered in a grand coil behind. But for the flowing skirt below, she might be mistaken for a young mid, whose cheeks as yet show only the down—one who would " find sweethearts in every port."

Miss Lees is less nautically attired; having but slipped over her morning dress a paletot of the ordinary kind, and on her head a plumed hat of the Neapolitan pattern. For all, a costume becoming; especially the brigand-like head-gear which sets off her finely-chiselled features, and skin dark as any daughter of the South.

They are about starting towards the boat-dock, when a difficulty presents itself —not to Gwen, but the companion.

"We have forgotten Joseph!" she exclaims.

Joseph is an ancient retainer of the Wynn family, who, in its domestic affairs, plays parts of many kinds—among them the *métier* of boatman. It is his duty to look after the *Gwendoline*, see that she is snug in her dock, with oars and steering apparatus in order; go out with her when his young mistress takes a row on the river, or ferry any one of the family who has occasion to cross it—the last a need by no means rare, since for miles above and below there is nothing in the shape of bridge.

D 2

"No, we haven't," rejoins Joseph's mistress, answering the exclamation of the companion. "I remembered him well enough—too well."

"Why too well?" asks the other, looking a little puzzled.

"Because we don't want him."

"But surely, Gwen, you wouldn't think of our going alone."

"Surely I would, and do. Why not?"

"We've never done so before."

"Is that any reason we shouldn't now?"

"But Miss Linton will be displeased, if not very angry. Besides, as you know, there may be danger on the river."

For a short while Gwen is silent, as if pondering on what the other has said. Not on the suggested danger. She is far from being daunted by that. But Miss Linton is her aunt—as already hinted, her legal guardian till of age—head of the house, and still holding authority, though exercising it in the mildest manner. And just on this account it would not be right to outrage it, nor is Miss Wynn the one to do so. Instead, she prefers a little subterfuge, which is in her mind as she makes re-joinder—

"I suppose we must take him along; though it's very vexatious, and for various reasons."

"What are they? May I know them?"

"You're welcome. For one, I can pull a boat just as well as he, if not better. And for another, we can't have a word of conversation without his hearing it—which isn't at all nice, besides being inconvenient. As I've reason to know, the old curmudgeon is an incorrigible gossip, and tattles all over the parish, I only wish we'd some one else. What a pity I haven't a brother, to go with us! *But not to-day.*"

The reserving clause, despite its earnestness, is not spoken aloud. In the aquatic excursion intended, she wants no companion of the male kind—above all, no brother. Nor will she take Joseph; though she signifies her consent to it, by desiring the companion to summon him.

As the latter starts off for the stable-yard, where the ferryman is usually to be found, Gwen says, in soliloquy—

" I'll take old Joe as far as the boat stairs; but not a yard beyond. I know what will stay him there—steady as a pointer with a partridge six feet from its nose. By the way, have I got my purse with me ? "

She plunges her hand into one of her pea-jacket pockets; and, there feeling the thing sought for, is satisfied.

By this Miss Lees has got back, bringing with her the versatile Joseph—a tough old servitor of the respectable family type, who has seen some sixty summers, more or less.

After a short colloquy, with some questions as to the condition of the pleasure-boat, its oars, and steering gear, the three proceed in the direction of the dock.

Arrived at the bottom of the boat stairs, Joseph's mistress, turning to him, says—

" Joe, old boy, Miss Lees and I are going for a row. But, as the day's fine, and the water smooth as glass, there's no need for our having you along with us. So you can stay here till we return."

The venerable retainer is taken aback by the proposal. He has never listened to the like before; for never before has the pleasure-boat gone to river without his being aboard. True, it is no business of his; still, as an ancient upholder of the family, with its honour and safety, he cannot assent to this strange innovation with out entering protest. He does so, asking :

" But, Miss Gwen ; what will your aunt say to it? She mayent like you young ladies to go rowin' by yourselves? Besides, Miss, ye know there be some not werry nice people as moat meet ye on the river. 'Deed some v' the roughiest and worst o' blaggarts."

"Nonsense, Joseph! The Wye isn't the Niger, where we might expect the fate of poor Mungo Park. Why, man, we'll be as safe on it as upon our own carriage drive, or the little fish-pond. As for aunt, she won't say anything, because she won't know.

Shan't, can't, unless you peach on us. The
which, my amiable Joseph, you'll not do—
I'm sure you will not ? "

"How'm I to help it, Miss Gwen?
When you've goed off, some o' the house
sarvints 'll see me here, an,' hows'ever I
keep my tongue in check——"

"Check it now ! " abruptly breaks in the
heiress, " and stop palavering, Joe! The
house servants won't see you—not one of
them. When we're off on the river, you'll
be lying at anchor in those laurel bushes
above. And to keep you to your anchorage,
here's some shining metal."

Saying which, she slips several shillings
into his hand, adding, as she notes the
effect,

" Do you think it sufficiently heavy ? If
not—but never mind now. In our absence
you can amuse yourself weighing, and
counting the coins. I fancy they'll do."

She is sure of it, knowing the man's
weakness to be money, as it now proves.

Her argument is too powerful for his
resistance, and he does not resist. De-

spite his solicitude for the welfare of the Wynn family, with his habitual regard of duty, the ancient servitor, refraining from further protest, proceeds ·to undo the knot of the *Gwendoline's* painter.

Stepping into the boat, the other Gwendoline takes the oars, Miss Lees seating herself to steer.

" All right! Now, Joe, give us a push off."

Joseph, having let all loose, does as directed; which sends the light craft clear out of its dock. Then, standing on the bottom step, with an adroit twirl of the thumb, he spreads the silver pieces over his palm—so that he may see how many— and, after counting and contemplating with pleased expression, slips them into his pocket, muttering to himself—

" I dar say it'll be all right. Miss Gwen's a oner to take care o' herself; an' the old lady neen't a know anythin' about it."

To make his last words good, he mounts briskly back up the boat stairs, and en-

sconces himself in the heart of a thick-
leaved laurestinus—to the great discomfort
of a pair of missel-thrushes, which have
there made nest, and commenced incuba-
tion.

CHAPTER IV.

THE fair rower, vigorously bending to the oars, soon brings through the bye-way, and out into the main channel of the river.

Once in mid-stream, she suspends her stroke, permitting the boat to drift down with the current; which, for a mile below Llangorren, flows gently through meadow land, but a few feet above its own level, and flush with it in times of flood.

On this particular day there is none such —no rain having fallen for a week—and the Wye's water is pure and clear. Smooth, too, as the surface of a mirror; only where, now and then, a light zephyr, playing upon it, stirs up the tiniest of ripples; a swallow dips its scimitar wings; or a salmon in bolder dash causes a purl, with circling eddies, whose wavelets extend wider and

wider as they subside. So, with the trace
of their boat's keel; the furrow made by it
instantly closing up, and the current resuming its tranquillity; while their reflected
forms—too bright to be spoken of as
shadows—now fall on one side, now on the
other, as the capricious curving of the river
makes necessary a change of course.

Never went boat down the Wye carrying
freight more fair. Both girls are beautiful,
though of opposite types, and in a different
degree; while with one—Gwendoline Wynn
—no water Nymph, or Naiad, could compare; her warm beauty in its real embodi-
ment far excelling any conception of fancy,
or flight of the most romantic imagination.

She is not thinking of herself now; nor,
indeed, does she much at any time—least
of all in this wise. She is anything but
vain; instead, like Vivian Ryecroft, rather
underrates herself. And possibly more than
ever this morning; for it is with him her
thoughts are occupied—surmising whether
his may be with her, but not in the most
sanguine hope. Such a man must have

looked on many a form fair as hers, won
smiles of many a woman beautiful as she.
How can she expect him to have resisted,
or that his heart is still whole ?

While thus conjecturing, she sits half
turned on the thwart, with oars out of
water, her eyes directed down the river, as
though in search of something there.
And they are; that something a white
helmet hat.

She sees it not; and as the last thought
has caused her some pain, she lets down
the oars with a plunge, and recommences
pulling; now, and as in spite, at each dip
of the blades breaking her own bright
image !

During all this while Ellen Lees is
otherwise occupied; her attention partly
taken up with the steering, but as much
given to the shores on each side—to the
green pasture-land, of which, at intervals,
she has a view, with the white-faced "Here-
fords" straying over it, or standing grouped
in the shade of some spreading trees, forming pastoral pictures worthy the pencil of a

Morland or Cuyp. In clumps, or apart,
tower up old poplars, through whose leaves,
yet but half unfolded, can be seen the
rounded burrs of the mistletoe, looking like
nests of rooks. Here and there, one over-
hangs the river's bank, shadowing still
deep pools, where the ravenous pike lies in
ambush for "salmon pink" and such small
fry; while on a bare branch above may be
observed another of their persecutors—the
kingfisher—its brilliant azure plumage in
strong contrast with everything on the
earth around, and like a bit of sky fallen
from above. At intervals it is seen darting
from side to side, or in longer flight following the bend of the stream, and causing
scamper among the minnows—itself startled
and scared by the intrusion of the boat
upon its normally peaceful domain.

Miss Lees, who is somewhat of a natu-
ralist, and has been out with the District
Field Club on more than one "ladies' day,"
makes note of all these things. As the
Gwendoline glides on, she observes beds of
the water ranunculus, whose snow-white

corollas, bending to the current, are oft
rudely dragged beneath; while on the
banks above, their cousins of golden sheen,
mingling with the petals of yellow and
purple loosestrife—for both grow here—
with anemones, and pale, lemon-coloured
daffodils—are but kissed, and gently fanned,
by the balmy breath of Spring.

Easily guiding the craft down the slow-
flowing stream, she has a fine opportunity
of observing Nature in its unrestrained
action—and takes advantage of it. She
looks with delighted eye at the freshly-
opened flowers, and listens with charmed
ear to the warbling of the birds—a chorus,
on the Wye, sweet and varied as anywhere
on earth. From many a deep-lying dell in
the adjacent hills she can hear the song of
the thrush, as if endeavouring to outdo,
and cause one to forget, the matchless strain
of its nocturnal rival, the nightingale; or
making music for its own mate, now on the
nest, and occupied with the cares of incu-
bation. She hears, too, the bold whistling
carol of the blackbird, the trill of the lark

soaring aloft, the soft sonorous note of the
cuckoo, blending with the harsh scream of
the jay, and the laughing cackle of the
green woodpecker—the last loud beyond all
proportion to the size of the bird, and bearing close resemblance to the cry of an eagle.
Strange coincidence besides, in the woodpecker being commonly called "eekol"—a
name, on the Wye, pronounced with striking
similarity to that of the royal bird !

Pondering upon this very theme, Ellen
has taken no note of how her companion
is employing herself. Nor is Miss Wynn
thinking of either flowers, or birds. Only
when a large one of the latter—a kite—
shooting out from the summit of a wooded
hill, stays awhile soaring overhead, does
she give thought to what so interests the
other.

"A pretty sight!" observes Ellen, as
they sit looking up at the sharp, slender
wings, and long bifurcated tail, cut clear as
a cameo against the cloudless sky. "Isn't
it a beautiful creature?"

"Beautiful, but bad;" rejoins Gwen,

"like many other animated things—too like, and too many of them. I suppose, it's on the look-out for some innocent victim, and will soon be swooping down at it. Ah, me! it's a wicked world, Nell, with all its sweetness! One creature preying upon another—the strong seeking to devour the weak—these ever needing protection! Is it any wonder we poor women, weakest of all, should wish to——"

She stays her interrogatory, and sits in silence, abstractedly toying with the handles of the oars, which she is balancing above water.

"Wish to do what?" asked the other.

"Get married!" answers the heiress of Llangorren, elevating her arms, and letting the blades fall with a plash, as if to drown a speech so bold; withal, watching its effect upon her companion, as she repeats the question in a changed form. "Is it strange, Ellen?"

"I suppose not," Ellen timidly replies; blushingly too, for she knows how nearly the subject concerns herself, and half believes

the interrogatory aimed at her. "Not at
all strange," she adds, more affirmatively.
" Indeed very natural, I should say—that
is, for women who *are* poor and weak, and
really need a protector. But you, Gwen—
who are neither one nor the other, but
instead rich and strong, have no such need."

"I'm not so sure of that. With all my
riches and strength—for I am a strong
creature ; as you see, can row this boat almost
as ably as a man "—she gives a vigorous pull
or two, as proof, then continuing, "Yes ;
and I think I've got great courage too.
Yet, would you believe it, Nelly, notwithstanding all, I sometimes have a strange
fear upon me ? "

"Fear of what ? "

" I can't tell. That's the strangest part
of it; for I know of no actual danger.
Some sort of vague apprehension that now
and then oppresses me—lies on my heart,
making it heavy as lead—sad and dark as
the shadow of that wicked bird upon the
water. Ugh ! " she exclaims, taking her
eyes off it, as if the sight, suggestive of

evil, had brought on one of the fear spells she is speaking of.

"If it were a magpie," observes Ellen, laughingly, "you might view it with sus- picion. Most people do—even some who deny being superstitious. But a kite—I never heard of that being ominous of evil. No more its shadow; which as you see it there is but a small speck compared with the wide bright surface around. If your future sorrows be only in like proportion to your joys, they won't signify much. See! Both the bird and its shadow are passing away—as will your troubles, if you ever have any."

" Passing — perhaps, soon to return. Ha! look there. As I've said!"

This, as the kite swoops down upon a wood-quest, and strikes at it with out- stretched talons. Missing it, nevertheless; for the strong-winged pigeon, forewarned by the other's shadow, has made a quick double in its flight, and so shunned the deadly clutch. Still, it is not yet safe; its tree covert is far off on the wooded slope, and the tyrant continues the chase. But the hawk has its enemy too, in a game-keeper with his gun. Suddenly it is seen to suspend the stroke of its wings, and go whirling downward; while a shot rings out on the air, and the cushat, unharmed, flies on for the hill.

"Good!" exclaims Gwen, resting the oars across her knees, and clapping her hands in an ecstacy of delight. "The innocent has escaped!"

"And for that *you* ought to be assured, as well as gratified;" puts in the companion, "taking it as a symbol of yourself, and those imaginary dangers you've been dreaming about."

"True;" assents Miss Wynn, musingly, "but, as you see, the bird found a protector—just by chance, and in the nick of time."

"So will you; without any chance, and at such time as may please you."

"Oh!" exclaims Gwen, as if endowed with fresh courage. "I don't want one—not I! I'm strong to stand alone."

Another tug at the oars to show it. "No," she continues, speaking between the plunges, "I want no protector—at least not yet—nor for a long while."

"But there's one wants you," says the companion, accompanying her words with an interrogative glance. "And soon— soon as he can have you."

"Indeed! I suppose you mean Master George Shenstone. Have I hit the nail upon the head?"

"You have."

"Well; what of him?"

"Only that everybody observes his attentions to you."

"Everybody is a very busy body. Being so observant, I wonder if this everybody has also observed how I receive them?"

"Indeed, yes."

"How then?"

"With favour. 'Tis said you think highly of him."

"And so I do. There are worse men in the world than George Shenstone—possibly ew better. And many a good woman

would, and might, be glad to become his
wife.   For all, I know one of a very
indifferent sort who wouldn't—that's Gwen
Wynn."

"But he's very good-looking?" Ellen
urges; "the handsomest gentleman in the
neighbourhood.   Everybody says so."

"There your everybody would be wrong
again—if they thought as they say. But
they don't. I know one who thinks somebody else much handsomer than he."

"Who?" asks Miss Lees, looking
puzzled.   For she has never heard of
Gwendoline having a preference, save that
spoken of.

"The Rev. William Musgrave," replies
Gwen, in turn bending inquisitive eyes on
her companion, to whose cheeks the answer
has brought a flush of colour, with a spasm
of pain at the heart.   Is it possible her rich
relative—the heiress of Llangorren Court
—can have set her eyes upon the poor
curate of Llangorren Church, where her
own thoughts have been secretly straying?
With an effort to conceal them now, as the

pain caused her, she rejoins interrogatively, but in faltering tone—

"You think Mr. Musgrave handsomer than Mr. Shenstone?"

"Indeed I don't. Who says I do?"

"Oh—I thought," stammers out the other, relieved—too pleased just then to stand up for the superiority of the curate's personal appearance — "I thought you meant it that way."

"But I didn't. All I said was, that somebody thinks so; and that isn't I. Shall I tell you who it is?"

Ellen's heart is again quiet; she does not need to be told, already divining who it is —herself.

"You may as well let me," pursues Gwen, in a bantering way. "Do you suppose, Miss Lees, I haven't penetrated your secret long ago? Why, I knew it last Christmas, when you were assisting his demure reverence to decorate the church! Who could fail to observe that pretty hand play, when you two were twining the ivy around the altar-rail? And the holly, you were both

so careless in handling—I wonder it didn't
prick your fingers to the bone ! Why, Nell,
'twas as plain to me, as if I'd been at it
myself. Besides, I've seen the same thing
scores of times—so has everybody in the
parish. Ha ! you see, I'm not the only one
with whose name this everybody has been
busy; the difference being, that about me
they've been mistaken, while concerning
yourself they haven't; instead, speaking
pretty near the truth. Come, now, confess!
Am I not right ? Don't have any fear, you
can trust me."

She does confess; though not in words.
Her silence is equally eloquent; drooping
eyelids, and blushing cheeks, making that
eloquence emphatic. She loves Mr. Musgrave.

"Enough !" says Gwendoline, taking it
in this sense ; "and, since you've been candid
with me, I'll repay you in the same coin.
But mind you ; it mustn't go further."

"Oh! certainly not," assents the other,
in her restored confidence about the curate,
willing to promise anything in the world.

"As I've said," proceeds Miss Wynn, "there are worse men in the world than George Shenstone, and but few better. Certainly none behind hounds, and I'm told he's the crack shot of the county, and the best billiard player of his club. All accomplishments that have weight with us women—some of us. More still; he's deemed good-looking, and is, as you say; known to be of good family and fortune. For all, he lacks one thing that's wanted by——"

She stays her speech till dipping the oars—their splash, simultaneous with, and half-drowning, the words, " Gwen Wynn."

"What is it?" asks Ellen, referring to the deficiency thus hinted at.

"On my word, I can't tell—for the life of me I cannot. It's something undefinable; which one feels without seeing or being able to explain—just as ether, or electricity. Possibly it is the last. At all events, it's the thing that makes us women fall in love; as no doubt you've found when your fingers were—were—well, so near being pricked by that holly. Ha, ha, ha!"

With a merry peal she once more sets to
rowing; and for a time no speech passes
between them—the only sounds heard being
the songs of the birds, in sweet symphony
with the rush of the water along the boat's
sides, and the rumbling of the oars in their
rowlocks.

But for a brief interval is there silence
between them; Miss Wynn again breaking
it by a startled exclamation :—

"See !"

"Where ? where ?"

"Up yonder! We've been talking of
kites and magpies. Behold, two birds of
worse augury than either !"

They are passing the mouth of a little
influent stream, up which at some distance
are seen two men, one of them seated in a
small boat, the other standing on the bank,
talking down to him. He in the boat is
a stout, thick-set fellow in velveteens and
coarse fur cap, the one above a spare thin
man, habited in a suit of black—of clerical,
or rather sacerdotal, cut. Though both are
partially screened by the foliage, the little

stream running between wooded banks,
Miss Wynn has recognised them. So, too,
does the companion; who rejoins, as if
speaking to herself—

"One's the French priest who has a
chapel up the river, on the opposite side;
the other's that fellow who's said to be such
an incorrigible poacher."

"Priest and poacher it is! An oddly-
assorted pair; though in a sense not so ill-
matched either. I wonder what they're
about up there, with their heads so close
together. They appeared as if not wishing
we should see them! Didn't it strike you
so, Nelly?"

The men are now out of sight; the boat
having passed the rivulet's mouth.

"Indeed, yes," answered Miss Lees;
"the priest, at all events. He drew back
among the bushes on seeing us."

"I'm sure his reverence is welcome. I've
no desire ever to set eyes on him—quite the
contrary."

"I often meet him on the roads."

"I too—and off them. He seems to be

about everywhere skulking and prying into people's affairs. I noticed him, the last day of our hunting, among the rabble— on foot, of course. He was close to my horse, and kept watching me out of his owlish eyes, all the time; so impertinently I could have laid the whip over his shoulders. There's something repulsive about the man; I can't bear the sight of him."

"He's said to be a great friend and very intimate associate of your worthy cousin, Mr. ——."

"Don't name *him*, Nell! I'd rather not think, much less talk of him. Almost the last words my father ever spoke—never to let Lewin Murdock cross the threshold of Llangorren. No doubt, he had his reasons. My word! this day with all its sunny brightness seems to abound in dark omens. Birds of prey, priests, and poachers! It's enough to bring on one of my fear fits. I now rather regret leaving Joseph behind. Well; we must make haste, and get home again."

"Shall I turn the boat back?" asks the steerer.

"No; not just yet. I don't wish to repass those two uncanny creatures. Better leave them awhile, so that on returning we mayn't see them, to disturb the priest's equanimity—more like his conscience."

The reason is not exactly as assigned; but Miss Lees, accepting it without suspicion, holds the tiller cords so as to keep the course on down stream.

CHAPTER V.

For another half mile, or so, the *Gwendoline* is propelled onward, though not running trimly; the fault being in her at the oars. With thoughts still preoccupied, she now and then forgets her stroke, or gives it un-equally—so that the boat zig-zags from side to side, and, but for a more careful hand at the tiller, would bring up against the bank.

Observing her abstraction, as also her frequent turning to look down the river—but without suspicion of what is causing it—Miss Lees at length inquires,

" What's the matter with you, Gwen ?"

" Oh, nothing," she evasively answers, bringing back her eyes to the boat, and once more giving attention to the oars.

"But why are you looking so often below? I've noticed you do so at least a score of times."

If the questioner could but divine the thoughts at that moment in the other's mind, she would have no need thus to interrogate, but would know that below there is another boat with a man in it, who possesses that unseen something, like ether or electricity, and to catch sight of whom Miss Wynn has been so oft straining her eyes. She has not given all her confidence to the companion.

Not receiving immediate answer, Ellen again asks—

"Is there any danger you fear?"

"None that I know of—at least, for a long way down. Then there are some rough places."

"But you are pulling so unsteadily! It takes all my strength to keep in the middle of the river."

"Then you pull, and let me do the steering," returns Miss Wynn, pretending to be in a pout; as she speaks starting up from the thwart, and leaving the oars in their thole pins.

Of course, the other does not object; and soon they have changed places.

But Gwen in the stern behaves no better, than when seated amidships. The boat still keeps going astray, the fault now in the steerer.

Soon something more than a crooked course calls the attention of both, for a time engrossing it. They have rounded an abrupt bend, and got into a reach where the river runs with troubled surface and great velocity—so swift there is no need to use oars down stream, while upward 'twill take stronger arms than theirs. Caught in its current, and rapidly, yet smoothly, borne on, for awhile they do not think of this. Only a short while; then the thought comes to them in the shape of a dilemma—Miss Lees being the first to perceive it.

" Gracious goodness ! " she exclaims, " what are we to do ? We can never row back up this rough water—it runs so strong here !"

" That's true," says Gwen, preserving her composure. " I don't think we could."

" But what's to be the upshot? Joseph will be waiting for us, and auntie sure to know all—if we shouldn't get back in time."

" That's true also," again observes Miss Wynn, assentingly, and with an admirable *sang froid*, which causes surprise to the companion.

Then succeeds a short interval of silence, broken by an exclamatory phrase of three short words from the lips of Miss Wynn. They are—" I have it !"

" What have you?" joyfully asks Ellen.

" The way to get back—without much trouble ; and without disturbing the arrangements we've made with old Joe—the least bit."

" Explain yourself !"

" We'll keep on down the river to Rock Weir. There we can leave the boat, and walk across the neck to Llangorren. It isn't over a mile, though it's five times that by the course of the stream. At the Weir we can engage some water fellow to take back the *Gwendoline* to her moorings. Meanwhile, we'll make all haste, slip into the grounds unobserved, get to the boat-dock in good time, and give Joseph the cue to hold his tongue about what's happened. Another half-crown will tie it firm and fast, I know."

" I suppose there's no help for it," says the companion, assenting, " and we must do as you say."

" Of course, we must. As you see, without thinking of it, we've drifted into a very cascade and are now a long way down it. Only a regular waterman could pull up again. Ah! 'twould take the toughest of them, I should say. So—*nolens volens*—we'll have to go on to Rock Weir, which can't be more than a mile now. You may feather your oars, and float a bit. But, by the way, I must look more carefully to the steering. Now, that I remember, there

are some awkward bars and eddies about
here, and we can't be far from them. I
think they're just below the next bend."

So saying, she sets herself square in the
stern sheets, and closes her fingers firmly
upon the tiller cords.

They glide on, but now in silence; the
little flurry, with the prospect of peril
ahead, making speech inopportune.

Soon they are round the bend spoken of,
discovering to their view a fresh reach of
the river; when again the steerer becomes
neglectful of her duty, the expression upon
her features, late a little troubled, suddenly
changing to cheerfulness, almost joy. Nor
is it that the dangerous places have been
passed; they are still ahead, and at some
distance below. But there is something
else ahead to account for the quick trans-
formation—a row-boat drawn up by the
river's edge, with men upon the bank
beside.

Over Gwen Wynn's countenance comes
another change, sudden as before, and as
before, its expression reversed. She has

mistaken the boat; it is not that of the handsome fisherman! Instead, a four-oared craft, manned by four men, for there is this number on the bank. The angler's skiff had in it only two—himself and his oarsman.

But she has no need to count heads, nor scrutinise faces. Those now before her eyes are all strange, and far from well favoured; not any of them in the least like the one which has so prepossessed her. And while making this observation another is forced upon her—that their natural plainness is not improved by what they have been doing, and are still—drinking.

Just as the young ladies make this observation, the four men, hearing oars, face towards them. For a moment there is silence, while they in the *Gwendoline* are being scanned by the quartette on the shore. Through maudlin eyes, possibly, the fellows mistake them for ordinary country lasses, with whom they may take liberties. Whether or not one cries out—

"Petticoats, by gee—ingo!"

"Ay!" exclaims another, "a pair o' them. An' sweet wenches they be, too. Look at she wi' the gooldy hair—bright as the sun itself. Lord, meeats! if we had she down in the pit, that head o' her ud gi'e as much light as a dozen Davy's lamps. An't she a bewty? I'm boun' to have a smack fra them red lips o' hers."

"No," protests the first speaker, "she be myen. First spoke soonest sarved. That's Forest law."

"Never mind, Rob," rejoins the other, surrendering his claim, "she may be the grandest to look at, but not the goodiest to go. I'll lay odds the black 'un beats her at kissin'. Le's get grup o' 'em an' see! Coom on, meeats!"

Down go the drinking vessels, all four making for their boat, into which they scramble, each laying hold of an oar.

Up to this time the ladies have not felt actual alarm. The strange men being evidently intoxicated, they might expect—

were, indeed, half-prepared for — coarse
speech; perhaps indelicate, but nothing
beyond. Within a mile of their own home,
and still within the boundary of the Llangorren land, how could they think of danger
such as is threatening? For that there is
danger they are now sensible—becoming
convinced of it, as they draw nearer to the
four fellows, and get a better view of them.
Impossible to mistake the men—roughs
from the Forest of Dean, or some other
mining district, their but half-washed faces
showing it; characters not very gentle at
any time, but very rude, even dangerous,
when drunk. This known, from many a
tale told, many a Petty and Quarter Sessions report read in the county newspapers.
But it is visible in their countenances, too
intelligible in their speech—part of which
the ladies have overheard—as in the action
they are taking.

They in the pleasure-boat no longer fear,
or think of, bars and eddies below. No
whirlpool—not Maelstrom itself, could fright
them as those four men. For it is fear of

a something more to be dreaded than drowning.

Withal, Gwendoline Wynn is not so much dismayed as to lose presence of mind. Nor is she at all excited, but cool as when caught in the rapid current. Her feats in the hunting field, and dashing drives down the steep "pitches" of the Herefordshire roads, have given her strength of nerve to face any danger; and, as her timid companion trembles with affright, muttering her fears, she but says—

"Keep quiet, Nell! Don't let them see you're scared. It's not the way to treat such as they, and will only encourage them to come at us."

This counsel, before the men have moved, fails in effect; for as they are seen rushing down the bank and into their boat, Ellen Lees utters a terrified shriek, scarcely leaving her breath to add the words—

"Dear Gwen! what shall we do?"

"Change places," is the reply, calmly but hurriedly made. "Give me the oars! Quick!"

While speaking she has started up from the stern, and is making for 'midships. The other, comprehending, has risen at the same instant, leaving the oars to trail.

By this the roughs have shoved off from the bank, and are making for mid-stream, their purpose evident—to intercept the *Gwendoline.* But the other Gwendoline has now got settled to the oars; and pulling with all her might, has still a chance to shoot past them.

In a few seconds the boats are but a couple of lengths apart, the heavy craft coming bow-on for the lighter; while the faces of those in her, slewed over their shoulders, show terribly forbidding. A glance tells Gwen Wynn 'twould be idle making appeal to them; nor does she. Still she is not silent. Unable to restrain her indignation, she calls out—

"Keep back, fellows! If you run against us, 'twill go ill for you. Don't suppose you'll escape punishment."

"Bah!" responds one, "we an't a-frightened at yer threats—not we. That

an't the way wi' us Forest chaps. Besides,
we don't mean ye any much harm. Only
gi'e us a kiss all round, an' then—maybe,
we'll let ye go."

" Yes ; kisses all round ! " cries another.
" That's the toll ye're got to pay at our
pike ; an' a bit o' squeeze by way o' boot."

The coarse jest elicits a peal of laughter
from the other three. Fortunately for
those who are its butt, since it takes the
attention of the rowers from their oars, and
before they can recover a stroke or two
lost—the pleasure-boat glides past them,
and goes dancing on, as did the fishing
skiff.

With a yell of disappointment they
bring their boat's head round, and row
after ; now straining at their oars with all
strength. Luckily, they lack skill; which,
fortunately for herself, the rower of the
pleasure-boat possesses. It stands her in
stead now, and, for a time, the *Gwendoline*
leads without losing ground. But the
struggle is unequal—four to one—strong
men, against a weak woman ! Verily is

she called on to make good her words, when saying she could row almost as ably as a man.

And so does she for a time. Withal it may not avail her. The task is too much for her woman's strength, fast becoming exhausted. While her strokes grow feebler, those of the pursuers seem to get stronger. For they are in earnest now; and, despite the bad management of their boat, it is rapidly gaining on the other.

" Pull, meeats ! " cries one, the roughest of the gang, and apparently the ringleader, " pull like—hic—hic ! "—his drunken tongue refuses the blasphemous word. " If ye lay me 'longside that girl wi' the gooc—goeeldy hair, I'll stan' someat stiff at the ' Kite's Nest ' whens we get hic—'ome."

" All right, Bob ! " is the rejoinder, " we'll do that. Ne'er a fear."

The prospect of " someat stiff " at the Forest hostelry inspires them to increase their exertion, and their speed proportionately augmented, no longer leaves a doubt of their being able to come up with the

pursued boat. Confident of it they commence jeering the ladies—"wenches" they
call them—in speech profane, as repulsive.

For these, things look black. They are
but a couple of boats' length ahead, and
near below is a sharp turn in the river's
channel; rounding which they will lose
ground, and can scarcely fail to be over-
taken. What then?

As Gwen Wynn asks herself the question, the anger late flashing in her eyes
gives place to a look of keen anxiety. Her
glances are sent to right, to left, and again
over her shoulder, as they have been all day
doing, but now with very different design.
Then she was searching for a man, with
no further thought than to feast her eyes
on him; now she is looking for the same,
in hopes he may save her from insult—it
may be worse.

There is no man in sight—no human
being on either side of the river! On the
right a grim cliff rising sheer, with some
goats clinging to its ledges. On the left
a grassy slope with browsing sheep, their

lambs astretch at their feet; but no shepherd, no one to whom she can call " Help ! "

Distractedly she continues to tug at the oars ; despairingly as the boats draw near the bend. Before rounding it she will be in the hands of those horrid men—embraced by their brawny, bear-like arms!

The thought restrengthens her own, giving them the energy of desperation. So inspired, she makes a final effort to elude the ruffian pursuers, and succeeds in turning the point.

Soon as round it, her face brightens up, joy dances in her eyes, as with panting breath she exclaims :—

" We're saved, Nelly ! We're saved ! Thank Heaven for it ! "

Nelly does thank Heaven, rejoiced to hear they are saved—but without in the least comprehending how !

CHAPTER VI.

Captain Ryecroft has been but a few minutes at his favourite fishing place—just long enough to see his tackle in working condition, and cast his line across the water; as he does the last, saying—

"I shouldn't wonder, Wingate, if we don't see a salmon to-day. I fear that sky's too bright for his dainty kingship to mistake feathers for flies."

"Ne'er a doubt the fish 'll be a bit shy," returns the boatman; "but," he adds, assigning their shyness to a different cause, "'tain't so much the colour o' the sky; more like it's that lot of Foresters has frightened them, with their hulk o' a boat makin' as much noise as a Bristol steamer. Wonder what brings such rubbish on the river anyhow. They han't no business on't;

an' in my opinion theer ought to be a
law 'gainst it—same's for trespassin' after
game."

"That would be rather hard lines, Jack.
These mining gentry need out-door recreation as much as any other sort of people.
Rather more I should say, considering that
they're compelled to pass the greater part
of their time underground. When they
emerge from the bowels of the earth to dis-
port themselves on its surface, it's but
natural they should like a little aquatics;
which you, by choice, an amphibious creature, cannot consistently blame them for.
Those we've just met are doubtless out for
a holiday, which accounts for their having
taken too much drink—in some sense an
excuse for their conduct. I don't think it
at all strange seeing them on the water."

"Their faces han't seed much o' it anyhow," observes the waterman, seeming little
satisfied with the Captain's reasoning.
"And as for their being out on holiday,
if I an't mistook, it be holiday as lasts
all the year round. Two o' 'em may be

miners—them as got the grimiest faces.
As for t'other two, I don't think eyther
ever touch't pick or shovel in their lives.
I've seed both hangin' about Lydbrook,
which be a queery place. Besides, one I've
seed 'long wi' a man whose company is
enough to gi'e a saint a bad character—
that's Coracle Dick. Take my word for 't,
Captain, there ain't a honest miner 'mong
that lot—eyther in the way of iron or coal.
If there wor I'd be the last man to go
again them havin' their holiday; 'cepting
I don't think they ought to take it on the
river. Ye see what comes o' sich as they
humbuggin' about in a boat?"

At the last clause of this speech—its
Conservatism due to a certain professional
jealousy—the Hussar officer cannot resist
smiling. He had half forgiven the rudeness of the revellers—attributing it to in-
toxication—and more than half repented
of his threat to bring them to a reckoning,
which might not be called for, but might,
and in all likelihood would be inconvenient.
Now, reflecting on Wingate's words, the

frown which had passed from off his face again returns to it. He says nothing, however, but sits rod in hand, less thinking of the salmon than how he can chastise the " d—d scoun'rels," as his companion has pronounced them, should he, as he antici- pates, again come in collision with them.

" Lissen ! " exclaims the waterman; " that's them shoutin' ! Comin' this way, I take it. What should we do to 'em, Cap- tain ? "

The salmon-fisher is half determined to reel in his line, lay aside the rod, and take out a revolving pistol he chances to have in his pocket—not with any intention to fire it at the fellows, but only frighten them.

" Yes," goes on Wingate, " they be drop- pin' down again—sure; I dar' say, they've found the tide a bit too strong for 'em up above. An' I don't wonder; sich louty chaps as they thinkin' they cud guide a boat 'bout the Wye ! Jist like mountin' hogs a-horseback ! "

At this fresh sally of professional spleen

the soldier again smiles, but says nothing, uncertain what action he should take, or how soon he may be called on to commence it. Almost instantly after he is called on to take action, though not against the four riotous Foresters, but a silly salmon, which has conceived a fancy for his fly. A purl on the water, with a pluck quick succeeding, tells of one on the hook, while the whizz of the wheel and rapid rolling out of catgut proclaims it a fine one.

For some minutes neither he nor his oarsman has eye or ear for aught save securing the fish, and both bend all their energies to "fighting" it. The line runs out, to be spun up and run off again; his river majesty, maddened at feeling himself so oddly and painfully restrained in his desperate efforts to escape, now rushing in one direction, now another, all the while the angler skilfully playing him, the equally skilled oarsman keeping the boat in concerted accordance.

Absorbed by their distinct lines of endeavour they do not hear high words, mingled

with exclamations, coming from above; or
hearing, do not heed, supposing them to
proceed from the four men they had met,
in all likelihood now more inebriated than
ever. Not till they have well-nigh finished
their "fight," and the salmon, all but subdued, is being drawn towards the boat—
Wingate, gaff in hand, bending over ready
to strike it. Not till then do they note
other sounds, which even at that critical
moment make them careless about the fish,
in its last feeble throes, when its capture is
good as sure, causing Ryecroft to stop
winding his wheel, and stand listening.

Only for an instant. Again the voices
of men, but now also heard the cry of a
woman, as if she sending it forth were in
danger or distress!

They have no need for conjecture, nor
are they long left to it. Almost simultaneously they see a boat sweeping round the
bend, with another close in its wake, evidently in chase, as told by the attitudes and
gestures of those occupying both—in the one
pursued two young ladies, in that pursuing

four rough men readily recognizable. At a glance the Hussar officer takes in the situation—the waterman as well. The sight saves a salmon's life, and possibly two innocent women from outrage. Down goes Ryecroft's rod, the boatman simultaneously dropping his gaff; as he does so hearing thundered in his ears—

"To yours oars, Jack! Make straight for them! Row with all your might!"

Jack Wingate needs neither command to act nor word to stimulate him. As a man he remembers the late indignity to himself; as a gallant fellow he now sees others submitted to the like. No matter about their being ladies; enough that they are women suffering insult; and more than enough at seeing who are the insulters.

In ten seconds' time he is on his thwart, oars in hand, the officer at the tiller; and in five more, the *Mary*, brought stem up stream, is surging against the current, going swiftly as if with it. She is set for the big boat pursuing—not now to shun a collision, but seek it.

As yet some two hundred yards are between the chased craft and that hastening to its rescue. Ryecroft, measuring the distance with his eyes, is in thought tracing out a course of action. His first instinct was to draw a pistol, and stop the pursuit with a shot. But no. It would not be English. Nor does he need resort to such deadly weapon. True there will be four against two; but what of it?

"I think we can manage them, Jack," he mutters through his teeth, "I'm good for two of them—the biggest and best."

"An' I t'other two—sich clumsy chaps as them! Ye can trust me takin' care o' 'em, Captin."

"I know it. Keep to your oars, till I give the word to drop them."

"They don't 'pear to a sighted us yet. Too drunk I take it. Like as not when they see what's comin' they'll sheer off."

"They shan't have the chance. I intend steering bow dead on to them. Don't fear the result. If the *Mary* get damaged I'll stand the expense of repairs."

" Ne'er a mind 'bout that, Captain. I'd gi'e the price o' a new boat to see the lot chestised—specially that big black fellow as did most o' the talkin'."

" You shall see it, and soon !"

He lets go the ropes, to disembarrass himself of his angling accoutrements ; which he hurriedly does, flinging them at his feet. When he again takes hold of the steering tackle the *Mary* is within six lengths of the advancing boats, both now nearly together, the bow of the pursuer overlapping the stern of the pursued. Only two of the men are at the oars ; two standing up, one amidships, the other at the head. Both are endeavouring to lay hold of the pleasure-boat, and bring it alongside. So occupied they see not the fishing skiff, while the two rowing, with backs turned, are equally unconscious of its approach. They only wonder at the " wenches," as they continue to call them, taking it so coolly, for these do not seem so much frightened as before.

" Coom, sweet lass !" cries he in the bow —the black fellow it is—addressing Miss

Wynn. "Tain't no use you tryin' to get away. I must ha' my kiss. So drop yer oars, and ge'et to me!"

"Insolent fellow!" she exclaims, her eyes ablaze with anger. "Keep your hands off my boat. I command you!"

"But I ain't to be c'mmanded, ye minx. Not till I've had a smack o' them lips; an' by G— I s'll have it."

Saying which he reaches out to the full stretch of his long, ape-like arms, and with one hand succeeds in grasping the boat's gunwale, while with the other he gets hold of the lady's dress, and commences dragging her towards him.

Gwen Wynn neither screams, nor calls "Help!" She knows it is near.

"Hands off!" cries a voice in a volume of thunder, simultaneous with a dull thud against the side of the larger boat, followed by a continued crashing as her gunwale goes in. The roughs, facing round, for the first time see the fishing skiff, and know why it is there. But they are too far gone in drink to heed or submit—at least their leader seems determined to resist. Turning savagely on Ryecroft, he stammers out—

"Hic—ic—who the blazes be you, Mr. White Cap! An' what d'ye want wi' me?"

"You'll see."

At the words he bounds from his own boat into the other; and, before the fellow can raise an arm, those of Ryecroft are around him in tight hug. In another minute the hulking scoundrel is hoisted from his feet, as though but a feather's weight, and flung overboard.

Wingate has meanwhile also boarded, grappled on to the other on foot, and is threatening to serve him the same.

A plunge, with a wild cry—the man going down like a stone; another, as he comes up among his own bubbles; and a third, yet wilder, as he feels himself sinking for the second time!

The two at the oars, scared into a sort of sobriety, one of them cries out—

"Lor' o' mercy! Rob'll be drownded! He can't sweem a stroke."

"He's a-drownin' now!" adds the other.

It is true. For Rob has again come to the surface, and shouts with feebler voice, while his arms tossed frantically about tell of his being in the last throes of suffocation!

Ryecroft looks regretful—rather alarmed In chastising the fellow he had gone too far. He must save him!

Quick as the thought off goes his coat, with his boots kicked into the bottom of the boat; then himself over its side!

A splendid swimmer, with a few bold sweeps he is by the side of the drowning man. Not a moment too soon—just as the latter is going down for the third—likely the last time. With the hand of the officer grasping his collar, he is kept above water. But not yet saved. Both are now imperilled —the rescuer and he he would rescue. For, far from the boats, they have drifted into a dangerous eddy, and are being whirled rapidly round!

A cry from Gwen Wynn—a cry of real alarm, now—the first she has uttered! But before she can repeat it, her fears are allayed

—set to rest again—at sight of still another rescuer. The young waterman has leaped back to his own boat, and is pulling straight for the strugglers. A few strokes, and he is beside them ; then, dropping his oars, he soon has both safe in the skiff.

The half-drowned, but wholly frightened, Bob is carried back to his comrades' boat, and dumped in among them ; Wingate handling him as though he were but a wet coal sack or piece of old tarpaulin. Then giving the "Forest chaps" a bit of his mind he bids them "be off!"

And off go they, without saying word ; as they drop down stream their downcast looks showing them subdued, if not quite sobered, and rather feeling grateful than aggrieved.

*   *   *   *   *   *

The other two boats soon proceed upward, the pleasure craft leading. But not now rowed by its owner ; for Captain Ryecroft has hold of the oars. In the haste, or the pleasurable moments succeeding, he has forgotten all about the salmon left struggling on his line, or caring not to

return for it, most likely will lose rod, line,
and all. What matter? If he has lost a
fine fish, he may have won the finest woman
on the Wye!

And she has lost nothing—risks nothing
now—not even the chiding of her aunt!
For now the pleasure-boat will be back in
its dock in time to keep undisturbed the
understanding with Joseph.

CHAPTER VII.

WHILE these exciting incidents are passing upon the river, Llangorren Court is wrapped in that stately repose becoming an aristocratic residence—especially where an elderly spinster is head of the house, and there are no noisy children to go romping about. It is thus with Llangorren, whose ostensible mistress is Miss Linton, the aunt and legal guardian already alluded to. But, though presiding over the establishment, it is rather in the way of ornamental figure-head; since she takes little to do with its domestic affairs, leaving them to a skilled house-keeper who carries the keys.

Kitchen matters are not much to Miss Linton's taste, being a dame of the antique brocaded type, with pleasant memories of the past, that go back to Bath and Chelten-

ham; where, in their days of glory, as hers
of youth, she was a belle, and did her share
of dancing, with a due proportion of flirt-
ing, at the Regency balls. No longer able
to indulge in such delightful recreations,
the memory of them has yet charms for her,
and she keeps it alive and warm by daily
perusal of the *Morning Post* with a fuller
hebdomadal feast from the *Court Journal*,
and other distributors of fashionable intel-
ligence. In addition she reads no end of
novels, her favourites being those which tell
of Cupid in his most romantic escapades
and experiences, though not always the
chastest. Of the prurient trash there is a
plenteous supply, furnished by scribblers of
both sexes, who ought to know better, and
doubtless do; but knowing also how difficult it is to make their lucubrations interesting within the legitimate lines of literary
art, and how easy out of them, thus trans-
gress the moralities.

Miss Linton need have no fear that the
impure stream will cease to flow, any more
than the limpid waters of the Wye. Nor

has she; but reads on, devouring volume after volume, in triunes as they issue from the press, and are sent her from the Circulating Library.

At nearly all hours of the day, and some of the night, does she so occupy herself. Even on this same bright April morn, when all nature rejoices, and every living thing seems to delight in being out of doors— when the flowers expand their petals to catch the kisses of the warm Spring sun, Dorothea Linton is seated in a shady corner of the drawing-room, up to her ears in a three-volume novel, still odorous of printer's ink and binder's paste; absorbed in a love dialogue between a certain Lord Lutestring and a rustic damsel—daughter of one of his tenant farmers—whose life he is doing his best to blight, and with much likelihood of succeeding. If he fail, it will not be for want of will on his part, nor desire of the author to save the imperilled one. He will make the tempted iniquitous as the tempter, should this seem to add interest to the tale, or promote the sale of the book.

Just as his lordship has gained a point and the girl is about to give way, Miss Linton herself receives a shock, caused by a rat-tat at the drawing-room door, light, such as well-trained servants are accustomed to give before entering a room occupied by master or mistress.

To her command " Come in ! " a footman presents himself, silver waiter in hand, on which is a card.

She is more than annoyed, almost angry, as taking the card, she reads—

" REVEREND WILLIAM MUSGRAVE."

Only to think of being thus interrupted on the eve of such an interesting climax, which seemed about to seal the fate of the farmer's daughter.

It is fortunate for his Reverence, that before entering within the room another visitor is announced, and ushered in along with him. Indeed the second caller is shown in first; for, although George Shenstone rung the front door bell after Mr. Musgrave had stepped inside the hall, there is no domestic of Llangorren but knows the difference between a rich baronet's son and a poor parish curate; as which should have precedence. To this nice, if not very delicate appreciation, the Reverend William is now indebted more than he is aware. It has saved him from an outburst of Miss Linton's rather tart temper, which, under the circumstances, otherwise he would have caught. For it so chances that the son of Sir George Shenstone is a great favourite with the old lady of Llangorren; welcome at all times, even amid the romantic gallantries of Lord Lutestring. Not that the young country gentleman has anything in common with the titled Lothario, who is habitually a dweller in cities. Instead, the former is a frank, manly fellow, devoted to field sports and rural pastimes, a little brusque in manner, but for all well-bred, and, what is even better, well behaved. There is nothing odd in his calling at that early hour. Sir George is an old friend of the Wynn family—was an intimate associate of Gwen's deceased father

—and both he and his son have been accustomed to look in at Llangorren Court *sans ceremonie.*

No more is Mr. Musgrave's matutinal visit out of order. Though but the curate, he is in full charge of parish duties, the rector being not only aged but an absentee —so long away from the neighbourhood as to have become almost a myth to it. For this reason his vicarial representative can plead scores of excuses for presenting himself at " The Court." There is the school, the church choir, and clothing club, to say nought of neighbouring news, which on most mornings make him a welcome visitor to Miss Linton; and no doubt would on this, but for the glamour thrown around her by the fascinations of the dear delightful Lutestring. It even takes all her partiality for Mr. Shenstone to remove its spell, and get him vouchsafed friendly reception.

" Miss Linton," he says, speaking first, " I've just dropped in to ask if the young ladies would go for a ride. The day's so fine, I thought they might like to.",

" Ah, indeed," returns the spinster, hold-
out her fingers to be touched, but, under
the plea of being a little invalided, excusing
herself from rising. " Yes ; no doubt they
would like it very much."

Mr. Shenstone is satisfied with the reply ;
but less the curate, who neither rides nor
has a horse. And less Shenstone himself—
indeed both—as the lady proceeds. They
have been listening, with ears all alert, for
the sound of soft footsteps and rustling
dresses. Instead, they hear words, not only
disappointing, but perplexing.

" Nay, I am sure," continues Miss Linton, with provoking coolness, "they would
have been glad to go riding with you;
delighted—"

" But why can't they ? " asked Shenstone,
impatiently interrupting.

" Because the thing's impossible ; they've
already gone rowing."

" Indeed ! " cry both gentlemen in a
breath, seeming alike vexed by the intelli-
gence, Shenstone mechanically interrogating :

"On the river?"

"Certainly!" answers the lady, looking surprised. "Why, George; where else could they go rowing! You don't suppose they've brought the boat up to the fish-pond!"

"Oh, no," he stammers out. "I beg pardon. How very stupid of me to ask such a question. I was only wondering why Miss Gwen—that is, I am a little astonished—but—perhaps you'll think it impertinent of me to ask another question?"

"Why should I? What is it?"

"Only whether — whether she — Miss Gwen, I mean—said anything about riding to-day?"

"Not a word—at least not to me."

"How long since they went off—may I know, Miss Linton?"

"Oh, hours ago! Very early, indeed—just after taking breakfast. I wasn't down myself—as I've told you, not feeling very well this morning. But Gwen's maid informs me they left the house then, and I presume they went direct to the river."

"Do you think they'll be out long?"
earnestly interrogates Shenstone.

"I should hope not," returns the ancient
toast of Cheltenham, with aggravating
indifference, for Lutestring is not quite out
of her thoughts. "There's no knowing,
however. Miss Wynn is accustomed to
come and go, without much consulting
me."

This with some acerbity—possibly from
the thought that the days of her legal
guardianship are drawing to a close, which
will make her a less important personage at
Llangorren.

"Surely, they won't be out all day,"
timidly suggests the curate; to which she
makes no rejoinder, till Mr. Shenstone puts
it in the shape of an inquiry."

"Is it likely they will, Miss Linton?"

"I should say not. More like they'll be
hungry, and that will bring them home.
What's the hour now? I've been reading
a very interesting book, and quite forgot
myself. Is it possible?" she exclaims,
looking at the ormolu dial on the mantel-

shelf. "Ten minutes to one! How time does fly, to be sure! I couldn't have believed it near so late—almost luncheon time! Of course you'll stay, gentlemen? As for the girls, if they're not back in time they'll have to go without. Punctuality is the rule of this house—always will be with me. I shan't wait one minute for them."

"But, Miss Linton; they may have returned from the river, and are now somewhere about the grounds. Shall I run down to the boat-dock and see?"

It is Mr. Shenstone who thus interrogates.

"If you like—by all means. I shall be too thankful. Shame of Gwen to give us so much trouble! She knows our luncheon hour, and should have been back by this. Thanks, much, Mr. Shenstone."

As he is bounding off, she calls after—

"Don't you be staying too, else you shan't have a pick. Mr. Musgrave and I won't wait for any of you. Shall we, Mr. Musgrave?"

Shenstone has not tarried to hear either

question or answer. A luncheon for Api-
cius were, at that moment, nothing to him;
and little more to the curate, who, though
staying, would gladly go along. Not from
any rivalry with, or jealousy of, the baronet's son : they revolve in different orbits,
with no danger of collision. Simply that
he dislikes leaving Miss Linton alone—
indeed, dare not. She may be expecting
the usual budget of neighbourhood intelli-
gence he daily brings her.

He is mistaken. On this particular day
it is not desired. Out of courtesy to Mr.
Shenstone, rather than herself, she had laid
aside the novel; and it now requires all
she can command to keep her eyes off it.
She is burning to know what befel the
farmer's daughter !

CHAPTER VIII.

WHILE Mr. Musgrave is boring the elderly spinster about new scarlet cloaks for the girls of the church choir, and other parish matters, George Shenstone is standing on the topmost step of the boat stair, in a mood of mind even less enviable than hers. For he has looked down into the dock, and there sees no Gwendoline—neither boat nor lady—nor is there sign of either upon the water, far as he can command a view of it. No sounds, such as he would wish, and might expect to hear—no dipping of oars, nor, what would be still more agreeable to his ear, the soft voices of women. Instead only the note of a cuckoo, in monotonous repetition, the bird balancing itself on a branch near by ; and, farther off, the *hiccol*, laughing, as if in mockery—and at him !

Mocking his impatience; ay, something more, almost his misery! That it is so his soliloquy tells :

"Odd her being out on the river! She promised me to go riding to-day. Very odd indeed! Gwen isn't the same she was —acting strange altogether for the last three or four days. Wonder what it means! By Jove, I can't comprehend it!"

His noncomprehension does not hinder a dark shadow from stealing over his brow, and there staying.

It is not unobserved. Through the leaves of the evergreen Joseph notes the pained expression, and interprets it in his own shrewd way—not far from the right one.

The old servant soliloquizing in less conjectural strain, says, or rather thinks—

"Master George be mad sweet on Miss Gwen. The country folk are all talkin' o't; thinkin' she's same on him, as if they knew anything about it. I knows better. An' he ain't no ways confident, else there wouldn't be that queery look on's face.

It's the token o' jealousy for sure. I don't
believe he have suspicion o' any rival par-
ticklar. Ah! it don't need that wi' sich
a grand beauty as she be. He as love
her might be jealous o' the sun kiss-
ing her cheeks, or the wind tossin' her
hair!"

Joseph is a Welshman of Bardic ancestry,
and thinks poetry. He continues—

" I know what's took her on the river, if
he don't. Yes—yes, my young lady! Ye
thought yerself wonderful clever leavin' old
Joe behind, tellin' him to hide hisself, and
bribin' him to stay hid! And d'y 'spose
I didn't obsarve them glances exchanged
twixt you and the salmon fisher—sly, but
for all that, hot as streaks o' fire? And
d'ye think I didn't see Mr. Whitecap going
down, afore ye thought o' a row yerself.
Oh, no; I noticed nothin' o' all that, not
I? 'Twarn't meant for me—not for Joe—
ha, ha!"

With a suppressed giggle at the popular
catch coming in so *apropos*, he once more
fixes his eyes on the face of the impatient

watcher, proceeding with his soliloquy, though in changed strain :

"Poor young gentleman ! I do pity he to be sure. He are a good sort, an' every-body likes him. So do she, but not the way he want her to. Well ; things o' that kind allers do go contrarywise—never seem to run smooth like. I'd help him myself if 'twar in my power, but it ain't. In such cases help can only come frae the place where they say matches be made—that's Heaven. Ha ! he's lookin' a bit brighter ! What's cheerin' him ? The boat coming back ? I can't see it from here, nor I don't hear any rattle o' cars ! "

The change he notes in George Shen-stone's manner is not caused by the return-ing pleasure craft. Simply a reflection which crossing his mind, for the moment tranquillizes him.

"What a stupid I am ! " he mutters self-accusingly. "Now I remember, there was nothing said about the hour we were to go riding, and I suppose she understood in the afternoon. It was so the last time we went out together. By Jove! yes. It's all right, I take it; she'll be back in good time yet."

Thus reassured he remains listening. Still more satisfied, when a dull thumping sound, in regular repetition, tells him of oars working in their rowlocks. Were he learned in boating tactics he would know there are two pairs of them, and think this strange too; since the *Gwendoline* carries only one. But he is not so skilled— instead, rather averse to aquatics—his chosen home the hunting field, his favourite seat in a saddle, not on a boat's thwart. It is only when the plashing of the oars in the tranquil water of the byeway is borne clear along the cliff, that he perceives there are two pairs at work, while at the same time he observes two boats approaching the little dock, where but one belongs!

Alone at that leading boat does he look; with eyes in which, as he continues to gaze, surprise becomes wonderment, dashed with something like displeasure. The boat he has recognized at the first glance—the

Gwendoline—as also the two ladies in the stern. But there is also a man on the mid thwart plying the oars.

" Who the deuce is he ? "

Thus to himself George Shenstone puts it. Not old Joe, not the least like him. Nor is it the family Charon who sits solitary on the thwarts of that following. Instead, Joseph is now by Mr. Shenstone's side, passing him in haste—making to go down the boat stairs !

" What's the meaning of all this, Joe? " asks the young man, in stark astonishment.

" Meanin' o' what, sir ? " returns the old boatman, with an air of assumed innocence. " Be there anythin' amiss ? "

" Oh, nothing," stammers Shenstone. " Only I supposed you were out with the young ladies. How is it you haven't gone ? "

" Well, sir, Miss Gwen didn't wish it. The day bein' fine, an' nothing o' flood in the river, she sayed she'd do the rowin' herself."

" She hasn't been doing it for all that,"

mutters Shenstone to himself, as Joseph glides past and on down the stair; then repeating, " Who the deuce is he?" the interrogation as before, referring to him who rows the pleasure boat.

By this it has been brought, bow in, to the dock, its stern touching the bottom of the stair; and, as the ladies step out of it, George Shenstone overhears a dialogue, which, instead of quieting his perturbed spirit, but excites him still more—almost to madness. It is Miss Wynn who has commenced it, saying.

" You'll come up to the house, and let me introduce you to my aunt?"

This to the gentleman who has been pulling her boat, and has just abandoned the oars soon as seeing its painter in the hands of the servant.

" Oh, thank you!" he returns. "I would, with pleasure; but, as you see, I'm not quite presentable just now—anything but fit for a drawing-room. So I beg you'll excuse me to-day."

His saturated shirt-front, with other garments dripping, tells why the apology ; but does not explain either that or aught else to him on the top of the stair; who, hearkening further, hears other speeches which, while perplexing him, do nought to allay the wild tempest now surging through his soul. Unseen himself—for he has stepped behind the tree lately screening Joseph—he sees Gwen Wynn hold out her hand to be pressed in parting salute—hears her address the stranger in words of gratitude, warm as though she were under some great obligation to him !

Then the latter leaps out of the pleasure boat into the other brought alongside, and is rowed away by his waterman ; while the ladies ascend the stair—Gwen, lingeringly, at almost every step, turning her face towards the fishing skiff, till this, pulled around the upper end of the eyot, can no more be seen.

All this George Shenstone observes, drawing deductions which send the blood in chill creep through his veins. Though still puzzled by the wet garments, the presence of the gentleman wearing them seems to solve that other enigma, unexplained as painful—the strangeness he has of late observed in the ways of Miss Wynn. Nor is he far out in his fancy, bitter though it be.

Not until the two ladies have reached the stair head do they become aware of his being there; and not then, till Gwen has made some observations to the companion, which, as those addressed to the stranger, unfortunately for himself, George Shenstone overhears.

"We'll be in time for luncheon yet, and aunt needn't know anything of what's delayed us—at least, not just now. True, if the like had happened to herself—say some thirty or forty years ago—she'd want all the world to hear of it, particularly that portion of the world yclept Cheltenham. The dear old lady! Ha, ha!" After a laugh, continuing: "But, speaking seriously, Nell, I don't wish any one to be the wiser about our bit of an escapade—least of all, a certain young gentleman, whose

Christian name begins with a G., and surname with an S."

"Those initials answer for mine," says
George Shenstone, coming forward and con-
fronting her. "If your observation was
meant for me, Miss Wynn, I can only ex-
press regret for my bad luck in being within
ear-shot of it."

At his appearance, so unexpected and
abrupt, Gwen Wynn had given a start—
feeling guilty, and looking it. Soon, however, reflecting whence he has come, and
hearing what said, she feels less self-con-
demned than indignant, as evinced by her
rejoinder.

"Ah! you've been overhearing us, Mr.
Shenstone! Bad luck, you call it. Bad
or good, I don't think you are justified in
attributing it to chance. When a gentleman deliberately stations himself behind a
shady bush, like that laurustinus, for instance, and there stands listening—inten-
tionally—"

Suddenly she interrupts herself, and
stands silent too—this on observing the

effect of her words, and that they have
struck terribly home. With bowed head
the baronet's son is stooping towards her,
the cloud on his brow telling of sadness—
not anger. Seeing it, the old tenderness
returns to her, with its familiarity, and she
exclaims:—

"Come, George! there must be no
quarrel between you and me. What you've
just seen and heard, will be all explained
by something you have yet to hear. Miss
Lees and I have had a little bit of an adventure; and if you'll promise it shan't go
further, we'll make you acquainted with
it."

Addressed in this style, he readily gives
the promise—gladly, too. The confidence
so offered seems favourable to himself.
But, looking for explanation on the instant,
he is disappointed. Asking for it, it is
denied him, with reason assigned thus:

"You forget we've been full four hours
on the river, and are as hungry as a pair of
kingfishers—hawks, I suppose, you'd say,
being a game preserver. Never mind

about the simile. Let us in to luncheon, if not too late."

She steps hurriedly off towards the house, the companion following, Shenstone behind both.

However hungry they, never man went to a meal with less appetite than he. All Gwen's cajoling has not tranquillized his spirit, nor driven out of his thoughts that man with the bronzed complexion, dark moustache, and white helmet hat.

CHAPTER IX.

CAPTAIN RYECROFT has lost more than rod and line; his heart is as good as gone too—given to Gwendoline Wynn. He now knows the name of the yellow haired Naiad—for this, with other particulars, she imparted to him on return up stream.

Neither has her confidence thus extended, nor the conversation leading to it, belied the favourable impression made upon him by her appearance. Instead, so strengthened it, that for the first time in his life he contemplates becoming a benedict. He feels that his fate is sealed—or no longer in his hands, but hers.

As Wingate pulls him on homeward, he draws out his cigar case, sets fire to a fresh weed, and, while the blue smoke wreaths up round the rim of his topee, reflects on the

incidents of the day,—reviewing them in
the order of their occurrence.

Circumstances apparently accidental have
been strangely in his favour. Helped as
by Heaven's own hand, working with the
rudest instruments. Through the veriest
scum of humanity he has made acquaintance with one of its fairest forms. More
than mere acquaintance, he hopes; for
surely those warm words, and glances far
from cold, could not be the sole offspring
of gratitude! If so, a little service on the
Wye goes a long way. Thus reflects he, in
modest appreciation of himself, deeming that
he has done but little. How different the
value put upon it by Gwen Wynn!

Still he knows not this, or at least cannot be sure of it. If he were, his thoughts
would be all rose-coloured, which they are
not. Some are dark as the shadows of the
April showers now and then drifting across
the sun's disc.

One that has just settled on his brow is
no reflection from the firmament above—no
vague imagining—but a thing of shape

and form—the form of a man, seen at the top of the boat stair, as the ladies were ascending, and not so far off as to have hindered him from observing the man's face, and noting that he was young, and rather handsome. Already the eyes of love have caught the keenness of jealousy. A gentleman evidently on terms of intimacy with Miss Wynn. Strange, though, that the look with which he regarded her on saluting, seemed to speak of something amiss! What could it mean! Captain Ryecroft has asked this question as his boat was rounding the end of the eyot, with another in the selfsame formulary of interrogation, of which but the moment before he was himself the subject :—

"Who the deuce can *he* be ? "

Out upon the river, and drawing hard at his Regalia, he goes on :—

" Wonderfully familiar the fellow seemed ! Can't be a brother ? I understood her to say she had none. Does he live at Llangorren ? No. She said there was no one there in the shape of masculine relative

—only an old aunt, and that little dark
damsel, who is cousin or something of the
kind. But who the deuce is the gentleman? Might *he* be a cousin?"

So propounding questions without being
able to answer them, he at length addresses
himself to the waterman, saying:

"Jack, did you observe a gentleman at
the head of the stair?"

"Only the head and shoulders o' one,
captain."

"Head and shoulders; that's enough.
Do you chance to know him?"

"I ain't thorough sure; but I think he
be a Mr. Shenstone."

"Who is Mr. Shenstone?"

"The son o' Sir George."

"Sir George! What do you know of *him?*"

"Not much to speak of—only that he be
a big gentleman, whose land lies along the
river, two or three miles below."

The information is but slight, and slighter
the gratification it gives. Captain Ryecroft
has heard of the rich baronet whose estate
adjoins that of Llangorren, and whose title,

with the property attached, will descend to
an only son. It is the *torso* of this son he
has seen above the red sandstone rock. In
truth, a formidable rival! So he reflects,
smoking away like mad.

After a time, he again observes :—

" You've said you don't know the ladies
we've helped out of their little trouble ? "

" Parsonally, I don't, captain. But, now
as I see where they live, I know who they
be. I've heerd talk 'bout the biggest o'
them—a good deal."

The biggest of them ! As if she were a
salmon ! In the boatman's eyes, bulk is
evidently her chief recommendation !

Ryecroft smiles, further interrogating :—

" What have you heard of her ? "

" That she be a *tidy* young lady. Wonderful fond o' field sport, such as hunting
and that like. Fr' all, I may say that up
to this day, I never set eyes on her afore."

The Hussar officer has been long enough
in Herefordshire to have learnt the local
signification of " tidy "—synonymous with
" well-behaved." That Miss Wynn is fond

of field sports—flood pastimes included—he
has 'gathered from herself while rowing her
up the river.

One thing strikes him as strange—that
the waterman should not be acquainted
with every one dwelling on the river's bank,
at least for a dozen miles up and down.
He seeks an explanation :—

"How is it, Jack, that you, living but a
short ·league above, don't know all about
these people ? "

He is unaware that Wingate, though
born on the Wye's banks, as he has told
him, is comparatively a stranger to its
middle waters—his birthplace being far up
in the shire of Brecon. Still, that is not
the solution of the enigma, which the young
waterman gives in his own way,—

"Lord love ye, sir ! That shows how
little you understand this river. Why,
captain ; it crooks an' crooks, and goes
wobblin' about in such a way, that folks as
lives less'n a mile apart knows no more o'
one the other than if they wor ten. It
comes o' the bridges bein' so few and far

between. There's the ferry boats, true ;
but people don't take to 'em more'n they
can help ; 'specially women—seein' there be
some danger at all times, and a good deal
o't when the river's a-flood. That's frequent, summer well as winter."

The explanation is reasonable ; and, satisfied with it, Ryecroft remains for a time
wrapt in a dreamy reverie, from which he is
aroused as his eyes rest upon a house—a
quaint antiquated structure, half timber,
half stone, standing not on the river's edge,
but at some distance from it up a dingle.
The sight is not new to him ; he has
before noticed the house—struck with its
appearance, so different from the ordinary
dwellings.

"Whose is it, Jack ? " he asks.

" B'longs to a man, name o' Murdock."

" Odd looking domicile ! "

" 'Ta'nt a bit more that way than he be
—if half what they say 'bout him be true."

" Ah ! Mr. Murdock's a character, then ? "

" Ay ; an' a queery one."

" In what respect ? what way ? "

"More'n one—a goodish many."

"Specify, Jack?"

"Well; for one thing, he a'nt sober to say half o' his time."

"Addicted to dipsomania?"

"'Dicted to getting dead drunk. I've seen him so, scores o' 'casions."

"That's not wise of Mr. Murdock."

"No, captain; 'ta'nt neyther wise nor well. All the worse, considerin' the place where mostly he go to do his drinkin'."

"Where may that be?"

"The Welsh Harp — up at Rogue's Ferry."

"Rogue's Ferry? Strange appellation! What sort of place is it? Not very nice, I should say—if the name be at all appropriate."

"It's parfitly 'propriate, though I b'lieve it wa'nt that way bestowed. It got so called after a man the name o' Rugg, who once keeped the Welsh Harp and the ferry too. It's about two mile above, a little ways back. Besides the tavern, there be a cluster o' houses, a bit scattered about, wi'

a chapel an' a grocery shop—one as deals
truckways, an' a'nt partickler as to what
they take in change—stolen goods welcome
as any—ay, welcomer, if they be o' worth.
They got plenty o' them, too. The place
be a regular nest o' poachers, an' worse
than that—a good many as have sarved
their spell in the Penitentiary."

"Why, Wingate, you astonish me! I
was under the impression your Wyeside
was a sort of Arcadia, where one only met
with innocence and primitive simplicity."

"You won't meet much o' either at
Rogue's Ferry. If there be an uninnocent
set on earth it's they as live there. Them
Forest chaps we came 'cross a'nt no ways
their match in wickedness. Just possible
drink made them behave as they did—some
o' 'em. But drink or no drink it be all the
same wi' the Ferry people—maybe worse
when they're sober. Any ways they're
a rough lot."

"With a place of worship in their midst!
That ought to do something towards refin-
ing them."

"Ought; and would, I dare say, if 'twar the right sort—which it a'nt. Instead, o' a kind as only the more corrupts 'em— being Roman."

"Oh! A Roman Catholic chapel. But how does it corrupt them?"

"By makin' 'em believe they can get cleared of their sins, hows'ever black they be. Men as think that way a'nt like to stick at any sort of crime—'specially if it brings 'em the money to buy what they calls absolution."

"Well, Jack; it's very evident you're no friend, or follower, of the Pope."

"Neyther o' Pope nor priest. Ah! captain; if you seed him o' the Rogue's Ferry Chapel, you wouldn't wonder at my havin' a dislike for the whole kit o' them."

"What is there specially repulsive about him?"

"Don't know as there be anythin' very special, in partickler. Them priests all look bout the same—such o' 'em as I've ever set eyes on. And that's like stoats and weasels, shootin' out o' one hole into another. As

for him we're speakin' about, he's here,
there, an' everywhere; sneakin' along the
roads an' paths, hidin' behind bushes like a
cat after birds, an' poppin' out where nobody expects him. If ever there war a spy
meaner than another it's the priest of
Rogue's Ferry."

"No?" he adds, correcting himself.
"There be one other in these parts worse
than he—if that's possible. A different
sort o' man, true; and yet they be a good
deal thegither."

"Who is this other?"

"Dick Dempsey—better known by the
name of Coracle Dick."

"Ah, Coracle Dick! He appears to
occupy a conspicuous place in your
thoughts, Jack; and rather a low one in
your estimation. Why, may I ask? What
sort of fellow is he?"

"The biggest blaggard as lives on the
Wye, from where it springs out o' Plin-
limmon to its emptying into the Bristol
Channel. Talk o' poachers an' night netters.
He goes out by night to catch somethin'

beside salmon. 'Taint all fish as comes into his net, I know."

The young waterman speaks in such hostile tone both about priest and poacher, that Ryecroft suspects a motive beyond the ordinary prejudice against men who wear the sacerdotal garb, or go trespassing after game. Not caring to inquire into it now, he returns to the original topic, saying :—

"We've strayed from our subject, Jack— which was the hard drinking owner of yonder house."

"Not so far, captain; seein' as he be the most intimate friend the priest have in these parts; though if what's said be true, not nigh so much as his Missus."

"Murdock is married, then?"

"I won't say that—leastwise I shouldn't like to swear it. All I know is, a woman lives wi' him, s'posed to be his wife. Odd thing she."

"Why odd?"

"'Cause she beant like any other o' womankind 'bout here."

"Explain yourself, Jack. In what does

Mrs. Murdock differ from the rest of your Herefordshire fair?"

"One way, captain, in her not bein' fair at all. 'Stead, she be dark complected; most as much as one o' them women I've seed 'bout Cheltenham, nursin' the children o' old officers as brought 'em from India— *ayers* they call 'em. She a'nt one o' 'em, but French, I've heerd say; which in part, I suppose explains the thickness 'tween her an' the priest—he bein' the same."

"Oh! His reverence is a Frenchman, is he?"

"All o' that, captain. If he wor English, he woudn't—coudn't—be the contemptible sneakin' hound he is. As for Mrs. Murdock, I can't say I've seed her more'n twice in my life. She keeps close to the house; goes nowhere; an' it's said nobody visits her nor him—leastwise none o' the old gentry. For all Mr. Murdock belongs to the best of them."

"He's a gentleman, is he?"

"Ought to be—if he took after his father."

" Why so?"

" Because he wor a squire—regular of the old sort. He's not been so long dead. I can remember him myself, though I hadn't been here such a many years—the old lady too—this Murdock's mother. Ah! now I think on't, she wor t'other squire's sister—father to the tallest o' them two young ladies—the one with the reddish hair."

" What! Miss Wynn?"

" Yes, captain; her they calls Gwen."

Ryecroft questions no farther. He has learnt enough to give him food for reflection—not only during the rest of that day, but for a week, a month—it may be throughout the remainder of his life.

CHAPTER X.

ABOUT a mile above Llangorren Court, but
on the opposite side of the Wye, stands the
house which had attracted the attention of
Captain Ryecroft; known to the neighbourhood as "Glyngog"—Cymric synonym for
"Cuckoo's Glen." Not immediately on the
water's edge, but several hundred yards
back, near the head of a lateral ravine which
debouches on the valley of the river, to the
latter contributing a rivulet.

Glyngog House is one of those habita-
tions, common in the county of Hereford
as other western shires—puzzling the stranger to tell whether they be gentleman's
residence, or but the dwelling of a farmer.
This from an array of walls, enclosing yard,
garden, even the orchard—a plenitude due
to the red sandstone being near, and easily
shaped for building purposes.

About Glyngog House, however, there is something besides the circumvallation to give it an air of grandeur beyond that of the ordinary farm homestead; certain touches of architectural style which speak of the Elizabethan period—in short that termed Tudor. For its own walls are not altogether stone ; instead a framework of oaken uprights, struts, and braces, black with age, the panelled masonry between plastered and white-washed, giving to the structure a quaint, almost fantastic, appearance, heightened by an irregular roof of steep pitch, with projecting dormers, gables acute angled, overhanging windows, and carving at the coigns. Of such ancient domiciles there are yet many to be met with on the Wye—their antiquity vouched for by the materials used in their construction, when bricks were a costly commodity, and wood to be had almost for the asking.

About this one, the enclosing stone walls have been a later erection, as also the pillared gate entrance to its ornamental grounds, through which runs a carriage drive to the sweep in front. Many a glittering equipage may have gone round on that sweep ; for Glyngog was once a Manor house. Now it is but the remains of one, so much out of repair as to show smashed panes in several of its windows, while the *enceinte* walls are only upright where sustained by the upholding ivy ; the shrubbery run wild ; the walks and carriage drive weed-covered ; on the latter neither recent track of wheel, nor hoof-mark of horse.

For all, the house is not uninhabited. Three or four of the windows appear sound, with blinds inside them ; while at most hours smoke may be seen ascending from at least two of the chimneys.

Few approach near enough the place to note its peculiarities. The traveller gets but a distant glimpse of its chimney-pots ; for the country road, avoiding the dip of the ravine, is carried round its head, and far from the house. It can only be approached by a long, narrow lane, leading nowhere else, so steep as to deter any explorer save a pedestrian ; while he, too, would have to contend with an obstruction of overgrowing thorns and trailing brambles.

Notwithstanding these disadvantages, Glyngog has something to recommend it— a prospect not surpassed in the western shires of England. He who selected its site must have been a man of tastes rather æsthetic, than utilitarian. For the land attached and belonging—some fifty or sixty acres—is barely arable; lying against the abruptly sloping sides of the ravine. But the view is superb. Below, the Wye, winding through a partially wood-covered plain, like some grand constrictor snake; its sinuosities only here and there visible through the trees, resembling a chain of detached lakes—till sweeping past the Cuckoo's Glen, it runs on in straight reach towards Llangorren.

Eye of man never looked upon lovelier landscape; mind of man could not contemplate one more suggestive of all that is, or ought to be, interesting in life. Peaceful smokes ascending out of far-off chimneys; farm-houses, with their surrounding walls,

standing amid the greenery of old homestead trees—now in full leaf, for it is the
month of June—here and there the sharp
spire of a church, or the showy façade of a
gentleman's mansion—in the distant back-
ground, the dark blue mountains of Mon-
mouthshire; among them conspicuous the
Blorenge, Skerrid, and Sugar Loaf. The
man who could look on such a picture,
without drawing from it inspirations of
pleasure, must be out of sorts with the
world, if not weary of it.

And yet just such a man is now viewing
it from Glyngog House, or rather the bit of
shrubbery ground in front. He is seated
on a rustic bench partly shattered, barely
enough of it whole to give room beside him
for a small japanned tray, on which are
tumbler, bottle and jug—the two last re-
spectively containing brandy and water;
while in the first is an admixture of both.
He is smoking a meerschaum pipe, which
at short intervals he removes from his mouth
to give place to the drinking glass.

The personal appearance of this man is

in curious correspondence with the bench on which he sits, the walls around, and the house behind. Like all these, he looks dilapidated. Not only is his apparel out of repair, but his constitution too, as shown by hollow cheeks and sunken eyes, with crows feet ramifying around them. This due not, as with the surrounding objects, to age; for he is still under forty. Nor yet any of the natural infirmities to which flesh is heir; but evidently to drink. Some reddish spots upon his nose and flecks on the forehead, with the glass held in shaking hand, proclaims this the cause. And it is.

Lewin Murdock—such is the man's name —has led a dissipated life. Not much of it in England; still less in Herefordshire; and only its earlier years in the house he now inhabits—his paternal home. Since boyhood he has been abroad, staying none can say where, and straying no one knows whither—often seen, however, at Baden, Homburg, and other "hells," punting high or low, as the luck has gone for or against him. At a later period in Paris, during the

Imperial *régime*—worst hell of all. It has stripped him of everything; driven him out and home, to seek asylum at Glyngog, once a handsome property, now but a *pied à terre*, on which he may only set his foot, with a mortgage around his neck. For even the little land left to it is let out to a farmer, and the rent goes not to him. He is, in fact, only a tenant on his patrimonial estate; holding but the house at that, with the ornamental grounds and an acre or two of orchard, of which he takes no care. The farmer's sheep may scale the crumbling walls, and browse the weedy enclosure at will; give Lewin Murdock his meerschaum pipe, with enough brandy and water, and he but laughs. Not that he is of a jovial disposition, not at all given to mirth; only that it takes something more than the pasturage of an old orchard to excite his thoughts, or turn them to cupidity.

For all, land does this—the very thing. No limited tract; but one of many acres in extent—even miles—the land of Llangorren.

It is now before his face, and under his

eyes, as a map unfolded. On the opposite side of the river it forms the foreground of the landscape; in its midst the many-windowed mansion, backed by stately trees, with well-kept grounds, and green pastures; at a little distance the "Grange," or home-farm, and farther off others that look of the same belonging—as they are. A smiling picture it is; spread before the eyes of Lewin Murdock, whenever he sits in his front window, or steps outside the door. And the brighter the sun shines on it, the darker the shadow on his brow!

Not much of an enigma either. That land of Llangorren belonged to his grandfather, but now is, or soon will be, the property of his cousin—Gwendoline Wynn. Were she not, it would be his. Between him and it runs the Wye, a broad deep river. But what its width or depth, compared with that other something between? A barrier stronger and more impassable than the stream, yet seeming slight as a thread. For it is but *the thread of a life*. Should it snap, or get accidentally severed, Lewin

Murdock would only have to cross the river, proclaim himself master of Llangorren, and take possession.

He would scarce be human not to think of all this. And being human he does—has thought of it oft, and many a time. With feelings too, beyond the mere prompting of cupidity. These due to a legend handed down to him, telling of an unfair disposal of the Llangorren property; but a pittance given to his mother who married Murdock of Glyngog; while the bulk went to her brother, the father of Gwen Wynn. All matters of testament, since the estate is unentailed; the only grace of the grandfather towards the Murdock branch being a clause entitling them to possession, in the event of the collateral heirs dying out. And of these but one is living—the heroine of our tale.

"Only she—but she!" mutters Lewin Murdock, in a tone of such bitterness, that, as if to drown it, he plucks the pipe out of his mouth, and gulps down the last drop in the glass.

CHAPTER XI.

" ONLY she—but she ! " he repeats, grasping the bottle by the neck, and pouring more brandy into the tumbler.

Though speaking *sotto voce*, and not supposing himself overheard, he is, nevertheless —by a woman, who, coming forth from the house, has stepped silently behind him, there pausing.

Odd-looking apparition she, seen upon the Wyeside ; altogether unlike a native of it, but altogether like one born upon the banks of the Seine, and brought up to tread the Boulevards of Paris—like the latter from the crown of her head to the soles of her high-heeled boots, on whose toes she stands poised and balancing. In front of that ancient English manor-house, she seems grotesquely out of place—as much as a costermonger driving his moke-drawn cart among the Pyramids, or smoking a "Pickwick" by the side of the Sphinx.

For all there is nothing mysterious, or even strange in her presence there. She is Lewin Murdock's wife. If he has left his fortune in foreign lands, with the better part of his life and health, he has thence brought her, his better-half.

Physically a fine-looking woman, despite some ravages due to time, and possibly more to crime. Tall and dark as the daughters of the Latinic race, with features beautiful in the past—even still attractive to those not repelled by the beguiling glances of sin.

Such were hers, first given to him in a *café chantant* of the Tuileries—oft afterwards repeated in *jardin*, *bois*, and *bals* of the demi-monde, till at length she gave him her hand in the Eglise La Madeleine.

Busied with his brandy, and again gazing at Llangorren, he has not yet seen her; nor is he aware of her proximity till hearing an exclamation :—

"*Eh, bien ?*"

He starts at the interrogatory, turning round.

" You think too loud, Monsieur—that is if you wish to keep your thoughts to yourself. And you might—seeing that it's a love secret! May I ask who is this *she* you're soliloquizing about? Some of your old English *bonnes amies*, I suppose?"

This, with an air of affected jealousy, she is far from feeling. In the heart of the *ex-cocotte* there is no place for such a sentiment.

"Got nothing to do with *bonnes amies*, young or old," he gruffly replies. "Just now I've got something else to think of than sweethearts. Enough occupation for my thoughts in the how I'm to support a wife—yourself, madame."

" It wasn't me you meant. No, indeed. Some other, in whom you appear to feel a very profound interest."

" There, you're right, it was one other, in whom I feel all that."

" *Merci, Monsieur! Ma foi!* your candour deserves all thanks. Perhaps you'll extend it, and favour me with the lady's name? A lady, I presume. The grand Seigneur Lewin Murdock would not be giving his thoughts to less."

Ignorance pretended. She knows, or surmises, to whom he has been giving them. For she has been watching him from a window, and observed the direction of his glances. And she has more than a suspicion as to the nature of his reflections; since she is well aware as he of that something besides a river separating them from Llangorren.

"Her name?" she again asks, in tone of more demand, her eyes bent searchingly on his.

Avoiding her glance, he still pulls away at his pipe, without making answer.

"It is a love secret, then? I thought so. It's cruel of you, Lewin! This is the return for giving you—all I had to give!"

She may well speak hesitatingly, and hint at a limited sacrifice. Only her hand; and it more than tenderly pressed by scores —ay hundreds—of others, before being bestowed upon him. No false pretence, however, on her part. He knew all that, or should have known it. How could he help? Olympe, the belle of the Jardin Mabille, was no obscurity in the *demi-monde* of Paris—even in its days of glory under Napoleon le Petite.

Her reproach is also a pretence, though possibly with some sting felt. She is drawing on to that term of life termed *passé*, and begins to feel conscious of it. He may be the same. Not that for his opinion she cares a straw—save in a certain sense, and for reasons altogether independent of slighted affection—the very purpose she is now working upon, and for which she needs to hold over him the power she has hitherto had. And well knows she how to retain it, rekindling love's fire when it seems in danger of dying out, either through appeal to his pity, or exciting his jealousy, which she can adroitly do, by her artful French ways and dark flashing eyes.

As he looks in them now, the old flame

flickers up, and he feels almost as much her
slave as when he first became her husband.

For all he does not show it. This day
he is out of sorts with himself, and her and
all the world besides ; so instead of recipro-
cating her sham tenderness—as if knowing
it such — he takes another swallow of
brandy, and smokes on in silence.

Now really incensed, or seeming so, she
exclaims :—

"*Perfide!*" adding with a disdainful toss
of the head, such as only the dames of the
demi-monde know how to give, "Keep your
secret! What care I?" Then changing
tone, "*Mon Dieu!* France—dear France!
Why did I ever leave you?"

"Because your dear France became too
dear to live in."

"Clever *double entendre!* No doubt you
think it witty! Dear, or not, better a
garret there—a room in its humblest *en-
tresol* than this. I'd rather serve in a cigar
shop—keep a *gargot* in the Faubourg Montmartre—than lead such a *triste* life as we're
now doing. Living in this wretched kennel

of a house, that threatens to tumble on our heads ! ”

“ How would you like to live in that over yonder ? ”

He nods towards Llangorren Court.

“ You are merry, Monsieur. But your jests are out of place—in presence of the misery around us.”

“ You may some day,” he goes on, without heeding her observation.

“ Yes ; when the sky falls we may catch larks. You seem to forget that Mademoiselle Wynn is younger than either of us, and by the natural laws of life will outlive both. Must, unless she break her neck in the hunting field, get drowned out of a boat, or meet *some other mischance.*”

She pronounces the last three words slowly and with marked emphasis, pausing after she has spoken them, and looking fixedly in his face, as if to note their effect.

Taking the meerschaum from his mouth, he returns her look—almost shuddering as his eyes meet hers, and he reads in them a glance such as might have been given by

Messalina, or the murderess of Duncan.
Hardened as his conscience has become
through a long career of sin, it is yet
tender in comparison with hers. And he
knows it, knowing her history, or enough
of it—her nature as well—to make him
think her capable of anything, even the
crime her speech seems to point to—neither
more nor less than—

He dares not think, let alone pronounce,
the word. He is not yet up to that;
though day by day, as his desperate fortunes press upon him, his thoughts are
being familiarized with something akin to
it—a dread, dark design, still vague, but
needing not much to assume shape, and
tempt to execution. And that the tempter
is by his side he is more than half conscious. It is not the first time for him to
listen to fell speech from those fair lips.

To-day he would rather shun allusion to
a subject so grave, yet so delicate. He has
spent part of the preceding night at the
Welsh Harp—the tavern spoken of by
Wingate—and his nerves are unstrung, yet

not recovered from the revelry. Instead of asking her what she means by "some other mischance," he but remarks, with an air of careless indifference,

"True, Olympe; unless something of that sort were to happen, there seems no help for us but to resign ourselves to patience, and live on expectations."

"Starve on them, you mean?"

This in a tone, and with a shrug, which seem to convey reproach for its weakness.

"Well, *cherie;*" he rejoins, "we can at least feast our eyes on the source whence our fine fortunes are to come. And a pretty sight it is, isn't it? *Un coup d'œil charmant!*"

He again turns his eyes upon Llangorren, as also she, and for some time both are silent.

Attractive at any time, the Court is unusually so on this same summer's day. For the sun, lighting up the verdant lawn, also shines upon a large white tent there erected —a marquee—from whose ribbed roof projects a signal staff, with flag floating at its peak. They have had no direct information of what all this is for—since to Lewin Murdock and his wife the society of Herefordshire is tabooed. But they can guess from the symbols that it is to be a garden party, or something of the sort, there often given. While they are still gazing its special kind is declared, by figures appearing upon the lawn and taking stand in groups before the tent. There are ladies gaily attired—in the distance looking like bright butterflies—some dressed *à la Diane*, with bows in hand, and quivers slung by their sides, the feathered shafts showing over their shoulders ; a proportionate number of gentlemen attendant ; while liveried servants stride to and fro erecting the ringed targets.

Murdock himself cares little for such things. He has had his surfeit of fashionable life; not only sipped its sweets, but drank its dregs of bitterness. He regards Llangorren with something in his mind more substantial than its sports and pastimes.

With different thoughts looks the Parisian upon them—in her heart a chagrin onl known to those whose zest for the world's pleasure is of keenest edge, yet checked and baffled from indulgence—ambitions uncontrollable, but never to be attained. As Satan gazed back when hurled out of the Garden of Eden, so she at that scene upon the lawn of Llangorren. No *jardin* of Paris—not the Bois itself—ever seemed to her so attractive as those grounds, with that aristocratic gathering—a heaven none of her kind can enter, and but few of her country.

After long regarding it with envy in her eyes, and spleen in her soul—tantalized, almost to torture—she faces towards her husband, saying—

" And you've told me, between all that and us, there's but one life——"

" Two ! " interrupts a voice—not his.

Both turning, startled, behold—*Father Rogier !*

CHAPTER XII.

FATHER ROGIER is a French priest of a type
too well known over all the world—the
Jesuitical. Spare of form, thin-lipped,
nose with the cuticle drawn across it tight
as drum parchment, skin dark and cadaver-
ous, he looks Loyola from head to heel.
He himself looks no one straight in the
face. Confronted, his eyes fall to his feet,
or turn to either side, not in timid abash-
ment, but as those of one who feels himself
a felon. And but for his habiliments he
might well pass for such; though even the
sacerdotal garb, and assumed air of sanctity,
do not hinder the suspicion of a wolf in
sheep's clothing — rather suggesting it.
And in truth is he one; a very Pharisee
—Inquisitor to boot, cruel and keen as

ever sate in secret Council over an *Auto da Fé*.

What is such a man doing in Hereford-shire? What, in Protestant England? Time was, and not so long ago, when these questions would have been asked with curiosity, and some degree of indignation. As for instance, when our popular Queen added to her popularity, by somewhat ostentatiously declaring, that "no foreign priest should take tithe or toll in her dominions," even forbidding them their dis-tinctive dress. Then they stole timidly, and sneakingly, through the streets, usually seen hunting in couples, and looking as if conscious their pursuit was criminal, or, at the least, illegal.

All that is over now; the ban removed, the boast unkept—to all appearance for-gotten! Now they stalk boldly abroad, or saunter in squads, exhibiting their shorn crowns and pallid faces, without fear or shame; instead, triumphantly flouting their vestments in public walks or parks, or loitering in the vestibules of convents and monasteries, which begin to show thick over the land—threatening us with a curse as that anterior to the time of bluff King Hal. No one now thinks it strange to see shovel-hatted priest, or sandalled monk— no matter in what part of England, nor would wonder at one of either being resi- dent upon Wyeside. Father Rogier, one of the former, is there with similar motive, and for the same purpose, his sort are sent everywhere—to enslave the souls of men and get money out of their purses, in order that other men, princes, and priests like himself, may lead luxurious lives, without toil and by trickery. The same old story, since the beginning of the world, or man's presence upon it. The same craft as the rain maker of South Africa, or the medi- cine man of the North American Indian; differing only in some points of practice; the religious juggler of a higher civiliza- tion, finding his readiest tools not in roots, snake-skins, and rattles, but the weakness of woman. Through this, as by sap and mine, many a strong citadel has been car-

ried, after bidding defiance to the boldest
and most determined assault.

Père Rogier well knows all this; and by
experience, having played the propagandist
game with some success since his settling
in Herefordshire. He has not been quite
three years resident on Wyeside, and yet
has contrived to draw around him a con-
siderable coterie of weak-minded Marthas
and Marys, built him a little chapel, with
a snug dwelling house, and is in a fair way
of further feathering his nest. True, his
neophytes are nearly all of the humbler
class, and poor. But the Peter's pence
count up in a remarkable manner, and are
paid with a regularity which only blind
devotion, or the zeal of religious partizan-
ship, can exact. Fear of the Devil, and
love of him, are like effective in drawing
contributions to the box of the Rugg's
Ferry chapel, and filling the pockets of its
priest.

And if he have no grand people among
his flock, and few disciples of the class
called middle, he can boast of at least two

claiming to be genteel—the Murdocks.
With the man no false assumption either;
neither does he assume, or value it. Different the woman. Born in the Faubourg
Montmartre, her father a common *ouvrier*,
her mother a *blanchisseuse*—herself a beautiful girl—Olympe Renault soon found her
way into a more fashionable quarter. The
same ambition made her Lewin Murdock's
wife, and has brought her on to England.
For she did not marry him without some
knowledge of his reversionary interest in
the land of which they have just been
speaking, and at which they are still looking. That was part of the inducement
held out for obtaining her hand; her heart
he never had.

That the priest knows something of the
same, indeed all, is evident from the word
he has respondingly pronounced. With
step, silent and cat-like—his usual mode of
progression — he has come upon them
unawares, neither having note of his
approach till startled by his voice. On
hearing it, and seeing who, Murdock rises

to his feet, as he does so saluting. Notwithstanding long years of a depraved life, his early training has been that of a gentleman, and its instincts at times return to him. Besides, born and brought up Roman Catholic, he has that respect for his priest, habitual to a proverb—would have, even if knowing the latter to be the veriest Pharisee that ever wore single-breasted black-coat.

Salutations exchanged, and a chair brought out for the new comer to sit upon, Murdock demands explanation of the interrupting monosyllable, asking:

"What do you mean, Father Rogier, by 'two'?"

"What I've said, M'sieu; that there are two between you and that over yonder, or soon will be—in time perhaps ten. A fair *paysage* it is!" he continues, looking across the river; "a very vale of Tempé, or Garden of the Hesperides. *Parbleu!* I never believed your England so beautiful. Ah! what's going on at Llangorren?" This as his eyes rest upon the tent, the flags, and gaily-dressed figures. "A *fête champétre :* Mademoiselle making merry! In honour of the anticipated change, no doubt."

"Still I don't comprehend," says Murdock, looking puzzled. "You speak in riddles, Father Rogier."

" Riddles easily read, M'sieu. Of this particular one you'll find the interpretation there."

This, pointing to a plain gold ring on the fourth finger of Mrs. Murdock's left hand, put upon it by Murdock himself on the day he became her husband.

He now comprehends—his quick-witted wife sooner.

"Ha!" she exclaims, as if pricked by a pin, " Mademoiselle to be married ? "

The priest gives an assenting nod.

"That's news to me," mutters Murdock, in a tone more like he was listening to the announcement of a death.

" *Moi aussi !* Who, *Père ?* Not Monsieur Shenstone, after all? "

The question shows how well she is acquainted with Miss Wynn—if not personally, with her surroundings and predilections !

" No," answers the priest. " Not he."

" Who then ? " asked the two simultaneously.

" A man likely to make many heirs to Llangorren—widen the breach between you and it—ah ! to the impossibility of that ever being bridged."

" *Père Rogier !* " appeals Murdock, " I pray you speak out ! Who is to do this? His name ? "

" *Le Capitaine Ryecroft.*"

" Captain Ryecroft ! Who—what is he ? "

" An officer of Hussars—a fine-looking fellow—sort of combination of Mars and Apollo ; strong as Hercules ! As I've said, likely to be father to no end of sons and daughters, with Gwen Wynn for their mother. *Helas !* I can fancy seeing them now—at play over yonder, on the lawn ! "

" Captain Ryecroft ! " repeats Murdock, musingly ; " I never saw—never heard of the man ! "

"You hear of him now, and possibly see him too. No doubt he's among those gay toxophilites—Ha! no, he's nearer! What a strange coincidence! The old saw, 'speak of the fiend.' There's *your* fiend, Monsieur Murdock!"

He points to a boat on the river with two men in it; one of them wearing a white cap. It is dropping down in the direction of Llangorren Court.

"Which?" asks Murdock, mechanically.

"He with the *chapeau blanc*. That's whom you have to fear. The other's but the waterman Wingate — honest fellow enough, whom no one need fear—unless indeed our worthy friend Coracle Dick, his competitor for the smiles of the pretty Mary Morgan. Yes, *mes amis!* Under that conspicuous *kepi* you behold the future lord of Llangorren."

"Never!" exclaims Murdock, angrily gritting his teeth. "Never!"

The French priest and ci-devant French courtezan exchange secret, but significant,

glances; a pleased expression showing on
the faces of both.

" You speak excitedly, M'sieu," says the
priest, " emphatically, too.   But how is it
to be hindered ? "

" I don't know," sourly rejoins Murdock ;
" I suppose it can't be," he adds, drawing
back, as if conscious of having committed
himself. " Never mind, now ; let's drop the
disagreeable subject.   You'll stay to dinner
with us, Father Rogier ? "

" If not putting you to inconvenience."

" Nay ; it's you who'll be inconvenienced
—starved, I should rather say. The butchers
about here are not of the most amiable type ;
and, if I mistake not, our *menu* for to-day is
a very primitive one—bacon and potatoes,
with some greens from the old garden."

" Monsieur Murdock ! It's not the fare,
but the fashion, which makes a meal enjoy
able. A crust and welcome is to me better
cheer than a banquet with a grudging host
at the head of the table. Besides, your
English bacon is a most estimable dish, and
with your succulent cabbages delectable. :

With a bit of Wye salmon to precede, and a pheasant to follow, it were food to satisfy Lucullus himself."

"Ah! true," assents the broken-down gentleman, "with the salmon and pheasant. But where are they? My fishmonger, who is, conjointly also a game-dealer, is at present as much out with me as is the butcher; I suppose, from my being too much in with them—in their books. Still, they have not ceased acquaintance, so far as calling is concerned. That they do with provoking frequency. Even this morning, before I was out of bed, I had the honour of a visit from both the gentlemen. Unfortunately, they brought neither fish nor meat; instead, two sheets of that detestable blue paper, with red lines and rows of figures—an arithmetic not nice to be bothered with at one's breakfast. So, *Père;* I am sorry I can't offer you any salmon; and as for pheasant—you may not be aware, that it is out of season."

"It's never out of season, any more than barn-door fowl; especially if a young last year's *coq*, that hasn't been successful in finding a mate."

"But it's close time now," urges the Englishman, stirred by his old instincts of gentleman sportsman.

"Not to those who know how to open it," returns the Frenchman, with a significant shrug. "And suppose we do that to-day?"

"I don't understand. Will your Reverence enlighten me?"

"Well, M'sieu ; being Whit-Monday, and coming to pay you a visit, I thought you mightn't be offended by my bringing along with me a little present—for Madame here —that we're talking of—salmon and pheasant."

The husband, more than the wife, looks incredulous. Is the priest jesting? Beneath the *froc*, fitting tight his thin spare form, there is nothing to indicate the presence of either fish or bird.

"Where are they?" asks Murdock mechanically. "You say you've brought them along?"

"Ah! that was metaphorical. I meant to say I had sent them. And if I mistake not, they are near now. Yes; there's my messenger!"

He points to a man making up the glen, threading his way through the tangle of wild bushes that grow along the banks of the rivulet.

"Coracle Dick!" exclaims Murdock, recognizing the poacher.

"The identical individual," answers the priest, adding, "who, though a poacher, and possibly has been something worse, is not such a bad fellow in his way—for certain purposes. True, he's neither the most devout nor best behaved of my flock; still a useful individual, especially on Fridays, when one has to confine himself to a fish diet. I find him convenient in other ways as well; as so might you, Monsieur Murdock — some day. Should you ever have need of a strong hard hand, with a heart in correspondence, Richard Dempsey possesses both, and would no doubt place them at your service—for a consideration."

While Murdock is cogitating on what the last words are meant to convey, the individual so recommended steps upon the ground. A stout, thick-set fellow, with a shock of black curly hair coming low down, almost to his eyes, thus adding to their sinister and lowering look. For all a face not naturally uncomely, but one on which crime has set its stamp, deep and indelible.

His garb is such as gamekeepers usually wear, and poachers almost universally affect, a shooting coat of velveteen, corduroy smalls, and sheepskin gaiters buttoned over thick-soled shoes iron-tipped at the toes. In the ample skirt pockets of the coat— each big as a game-bag—appear two protuberances, that about balance one another— the present of which the priest has already delivered the invoice—in the one being a salmon " blotcher " weighing some three or four pounds, in the other a young cock pheasant.

Having made obeisance to the trio in the grounds of Glyngog, he is about drawing them forth when the priest prevents him, exclaiming :—

"*Arretez!* They're not commodities that keep well in the sun. Should a water-bailiff, or one of the Llangorren gamekeepers chance to set eyes on them, they'd spoil at once. Those lynx-eyed fellows can see a long way, especially on a day bright as this. So, worthy Coracle, before uncarting, you'd better take them back to the kitchen."

Thus instructed, the poacher strides off round to the rear of the house; Mrs. Murdock entering by the front door to give directions about dressing the dinner. Not that she intends to take any hand in cooking it—not she. That would be *infra dig.* for the *ancien belle of Mabille.* Poor as is the establishment of Glyngog, it can boast of a plain cook, with a *slavey* to assist.

The other two remain outside, the guest joining his host in a glass of brandy and water. More than one; for Father Rogier, though French, can drink like a born Hibernian. Nothing of the Good Templar in him.

After they have been for nigh an hour hobnobbing, conversing, Murdock still fighting shy of the subject, which is nevertheless uppermost in the minds of both, the priest once more approaches it, saying :—

" *Parbleu!* They appear to be enjoying themselves over yonder!" He is looking at the lawn where the bright forms are flitting to and fro. " And most of all, I should say, Monsieur White Cap—foretasting the sweets of which he'll ere long enter into full enjoyment; when he becomes master of Llangorren."

" That—never!" exclaims Murdock, this time adding an oath. " Never while I live. When I'm dead——"

" *Diner!* " interrupts a female voice from the house, that of its mistress seen standing on the doorstep.

" Madame summons us," says the priest, " we must in, M'ssieu. While picking the bones of the pheasant, you can complete your unfinished speech. *Allons!* "

CHAPTER XIII.

THE invited to the archery meeting have nearly all arrived, and the shooting has commenced; half a dozen arrows in the air at a time, making for as many targets.

Only a limited number of ladies compete for the first score, each having a little coterie of acquaintances at her back.

Gwen Wynn herself is in this opening contest. Good with the bow, as at the oar —indeed with county celebrity as an archer —carrying the champion badge of her club —it is almost a foregone conclusion she will come off victorious.

Soon, however, those who are backing her begin to anticipate disappointment. She is not shooting with her usual skill, nor yet earnestness. Instead, negligently, and to all appearance, with thoughts abstracted; her eyes every now and then straying over the ground, scanning the various groups, as if in search of a particular individual. The gathering is large —nearly a hundred people present—and one might come or go without attracting observation. She evidently expects one to come who is not yet there ; and oftener than elsewhere her glances go towards the boat-dock, as if the personage expected should appear in that direction. There is a nervous restlessness in her manner, and after each reconnaissance of this kind, an expression of disappointment on her countenance.

It is not unobserved. A gentleman by her side notes it, and with some suspicion of its cause—a suspicion that pains him. It is George Shenstone; who is attending on her, handing the arrows—in short, acting as her *aide-de-camp*. Neither is he adroit in the exercise of his duty; instead performs it bunglingly; his thoughts pre-occupied, and eyes wandering about. His glances, however, are sent in the opposite direction—to the gate entrance of the park, visible from the place where the targets are set up.

They are both "prospecting" for the self-same individual, but with very different ideas— one eagerly anticipating his arrival, the other as earnestly hoping he may not come. For the expected one is a gentleman —no other than Vivian Ryecroft.

Shenstone knows the Hussar officer has been invited; and, however hoping or wishing it, has but little faith he will fail. Were it himself no ordinary obstacle could prevent his being present at that archery meeting, any more than would five-barred gate, or bullfinch, hinder him from keeping up with hounds.

As time passes without any further arrivals, and the tardy guest has not yet put in appearance, Shenstone begins to think he will this day have Miss Wynn to himself, or at least without any very formidable competitor. There are others present who seek her smiles—some aspiring to her hand— but none he fears so much as the one still absent.

Just as he is becoming calm, and confident, he is saluted by a gentleman of the
genus " swell," who, approaching, drawls
out the interrogatory :—

" Who is that fella, Shenstone ? "

" What fellow ? "

" He with the vewy peculya head gear ?
Indian affair—*topee*, I bewieve they call it."

" Where ? " asks Shenstone, starting and
staring to all sides.

" Yondaw ! Appwoaching from the
diwection of the rivaw. Looks a fwesh
awival. I take it, he must have come by
bawt ! Knaw him ? "

George Shenstone, strong man though he
be, visibly trembles. Were Gwen Wynn at
that moment to face about, and aim one of
her arrows at his breast, it would not bring
more pallor upon his cheeks, nor pain to his
heart. For he wearing the " peculya head
gear " is the man he most fears, and whom
he had hoped not to see this day.

So much is he affected, he does not
answer the question put to him ; nor indeed
has he opportunity, as just then Miss Wynn,

sighting the *topee* too, suddenly turning, says to him :—

" George ! be good enough to take charge of these things." She holds her bow with an arrow she had been affixing to the string. " Yonder's a gentleman just arrived ; who you know is a stranger. Aunt will expect me to receive him. I'll be back soon as I've discharged my duty."

Delivering the bow and unspent shaft, she glides off without further speech or ceremony.

He stands looking after ; in his eyes anything but a pleased expression. Indeed, sullen, almost angry, as watching her every movement, he notes the manner of her reception—greeting the new comer with a warmth and cordiality he, Shenstone, thinks uncalled for, however much stranger the man may be. Little irksome to her seems the discharge of that so-called duty ; but so exasperating to the baronet's son, he feels like crushing the bow stick between his fingers, or snapping it in twain across his knee !

As he stands with eyes glaring upon them, he is again accosted by his inquisitive acquaintance, who asks :

" What's the matter, Jawge? Yaw haven't answered my intewogatowy ! "

" What was it ? I forget."

" Aw, indeed ! That's stwange. I merely wished to knaw who Mr. White Cap is ? "

" Just what I'd like to know myself. All I can tell you is, that he's an army fellow —in the Cavalry I believe—by name Ryecroft."

" Aw yas ; Cavalwy. That's evident by the bend of his legs. Wyquoft—Wyquoft, you say ? "

" So he calls himself—a captain of Hussars—his own story."

This in a tone and with a shrug of insinuation.

" But yaw don't think he's an adventuwer ? "

" Can't say whether he is, or not."

" Who's his endawser ? How came he intwoduced at Llangowen ? "

"That I can't tell you."

He could though; for Miss Wynn, true to her promise, has made him acquainted with the circumstances of the river adventure, though not those leading to it; and he, true to his, has kept them a secret. In a sense therefore, he could not tell, and the subterfuge is excusable.

"By Jawve! The Light Bob appears to have made good use of his time—however intwoduced. Miss Gwen seems quite familiaw with him; and yondaw the little Lees shaking hands, as though the two had been acquainted evaw since coming out of their cwadles! See! They're dwagging him up to the ancient spinster, who sits enthawned in her chair like a queen of the Tawnament times. Vewy mediæval the whole affair—vewy!"

"Instead, very modern; in my opinion, disgustingly so!"

"Why d'yaw say that, Jawge?"

"Why! Because in either olden or mediæval times such a thing couldn't have occurred—here in Herefordshire."

" What thing, pway ? "

" A man admitted into good society without endorsement or introduction. Now-a-days, any one may be so; claim acquaintance with a lady, and force his company upon her, simply from having had the chance to pick up a dropped pocket-handkerchief, or offer his umbrella in a skiff of a shower ! "

" But, shawly, that isn't how the gentleman yondaw made acquaintance with the fair Gwendoline ? "

" Oh ! I don't say that," rejoins Shenstone with forced attempt at a smile—more natural, as he sees Miss Wynn separate from the group they are gazing at, and come back to reclaim her bow. Better satisfied, now, he is rather worried by his importunate friend, and to get rid of him adds :

" If you are really desirous to know how Miss Wynn became acquainted with him, you can ask the lady herself."

Not for all the world would the swell put that question to Gwen Wynn. It would not be safe ; and thus snubbed he saunters away, before she is up to the spot.

Ryecroft, left with Miss Linton, remains in conversation with her. It is not his first interview ; for several times already has he been a visitor at Llangorren—introduced by the young ladies as the gentleman who, when the pleasure-boat was caught in a dangerous whirl, out of which old Joseph was unable to extricate it, came to their rescue—possibly to the saving of their lives! Thus, the version of the adventure, vouchsafed to the aunt—sufficient to sanction his being received at the Court.

And the ancient toast of Cheltenham has been charmed with him. In the handsome Hussar officer she beholds the typical hero of her romance reading; so much like it, that Lord Lutestring has long ago gone out of her thoughts—passed from her memory as though he had been but a musical sound. Of all who bend before her this day, the worship of none is so welcome as that of the martial stranger.

*　　*　　*　　*　　*　　*

Resuming her bow, Gwen shoots no
better than before. Her thoughts, instead
of being concentrated on the painted
circles, as her eyes, are half the time straying over her shoulders to him behind, still
in a *téte-à-téte* with the aunt. Her arrows
fly wild and wide, scarce one sticking in
the straw. In fine, among all the competi-
tors, she counts lowest score—the poorest
she has herself ever made. But what
matters it? She is only too pleased when
her quiver is empty, and she can have
excuse to return to Miss Linton, on some
question connected with the hospitalities
of the house.

Observing all this, and much more
besides, George Shenstone feels aggrieved
—indeed exasperated—so terribly, it takes
all his best breeding to withhold him from
an exhibition of bad behaviour. He might
not succeed were he to remain much
longer on the ground—which he does not.
As if misdoubting his power of restraint,
and fearing to make a fool of himself, he
too frames excuse, and leaves Llangorren

long before the sports come to a close.
Not rudely, or with any show of spleen.
He is a gentleman, even in his anger; and
bidding a polite, and formal, adieu to Miss
Linton, with one equally ceremonious, but
more distant, to Miss Wynn, he slips round
to the stables, orders his horse, leaps into
the saddle, and rides off.

Many the day he has entered the gates
of Llangorren with a light and happy
heart—this day he goes out of them with
one heavy and sad.

If missed from the archery meeting, it is
not by Miss Wynn. Instead, she is glad
of his being gone. Notwithstanding the
love passion for another now occupying
her heart—almost filling it—there is still
room there for the gentler sentiment of pity.
She knows how Shenstone suffers—how
could she help knowing? and pities him.

Never more than at this same moment,
despite that distant, half disdainful adieu,
vouchsafed to her at parting; by him
intended to conceal his thoughts, as his
sufferings, while but the better revealing

them. How men underrate the perception of women ! In matters of this kind a very intuition.

None keener than that of Gwen Wynn. She knows why he has gone so short away ,—well as if he had told her. And with the compassionate thought still lingering, she heaves a sigh ; sad as she sees him ride out through the gate—going in reck. less gallop—but succeeded by one of relief, soon as he is out of sight !

In an instant after, she is gay and gladsome as ever; once more bending the bow, and making the catgut twang. But now shooting straight—hitting the target every time, and not unfrequently lodging a shaft in the " gold." For he who now attends on her, not only inspires confidence, but excites her to the display of skill. Captain Ryecroft has taken George Shenstone's place, as her aide-de-camp ; and while he hands the arrows, she spending them, others of a different kind pass between— the shafts of ¡Cupid—of which there is a full quiver in the eyes of both.

CHAPTER XIV

NATURALLY, Captain Ryecroft is the subject of speculation among the archers at Llangorren. A man of his mien would be so anywhere—if stranger. The old story of the unknown knight suddenly appearing on the tourney's field with closed visor, only recognizable by a love-lock or other favour of the lady whose cause he comes to champion.

He, too, wears a distinctive badge—in the white cap. For though our tale is of modern time, it antedates that when Brown began to affect the *pugaree*—sham of Manchester Mills—as an appendage to his cheap straw hat. That on the head of Captain Ryecroft is the regular forage cap with quilted cover. Accustomed to it in India —whence he has but lately returned—he adheres to it in England without thought of its attracting attention and as little caring whether it do or not.

It does, however. Insular, we are supremely conservative—some might call it "caddish"—and view innovations with a jealous eye ; as witness the so-called "moustache movement" not many years ago, and the fierce controversy it called forth.

For other reasons the officer of Hussars is at this same archery gathering a cynosure of eyes. There is a perfume of romance about him ; in the way he has been introduced to the ladies of Llangorren ; a question asked by others besides the importunate friend of George Shenstone. The true account of the affair with the drunken foresters has not got abroad—these keeping dumb about their own discomfiture; while Jack Wingate, a man of few words, and on this special matter admonished to silence, has been equally close-mouthed ; Joseph also mute for reasons already mentioned.

Withal, a vague story has currency in the

neighbourhood, of a boat, with two young ladies, in danger of being capsized—by some versions actually upset — and the ladies rescued from drowning by a stranger who chanced to be salmon fishing near by —his name, Ryecroft. And as this tale also circulates among the archers at Llangorren, it is not strange that some interest should attach to the supposed hero of it, now present.

Still, in an assemblage so large, and composed of such distinguished people—many of whom are strangers to one another—no particular personage can be for long an object of special concern; and if Captain Ryecroft continue to attract observation, it is neither from curiosity as to how he came there, nor the peculiarity of his head-dress, but the dark handsome features beneath it. On these more than one pair of bright eyes occasionally become fixed, regarding them with admiration.

None so warmly as those of Gwen Wynn; though hers neither openly nor in a marked manner. For she is conscious of being

under the surveillance of other eyes, and
needs to observe the proprieties.

In which she succeeds; so well, that no
one watching her could tell, much less say,
there is aught in her behaviour to Captain
Ryecroft beyond the hospitality of host—
which in a sense she is—to guest claiming
the privileges of a stranger. Even when
during an interregnum of the sports the two
go off together, and, after strolling for a
time through the grounds, are at length
seen to step inside the summer-house, it
may cause, but does not merit, remark.
Others are acting similarly, sauntering in
pairs, loitering in shady places, or sitting
on rustic benches. Good society allows the
freedom, and to its credit. That which is
corrupt alone may cavil at it, and shame
the day when such confidence be abused and
abrogated!

Side by side they take stand in the little
pavilion, under the shadow of its painted
zinc roof. It may not have been all chance
their coming thither—no more the archery
party itself. That Gwendoline Wynn, who

suggested giving it, can alone tell. But
standing there with their eyes bent on the
river, they are for a time silent—so much,
that each can hear the beating of the other's
heart—both brimful of love.

At such moment one might suppose there
could be no reserve or reticence, but confession full, candid, and mutual. Instead,
at no time is this farther off. If *le joie fait
peur*, far more *l'amour*.

And with all that has passed is there fear
between them. On her part springing from
a fancy she has been over forward—in her
gushing gratitude for that service done,
given too free expression to it, and needs
being more reserved now. On his side
speech is stayed by a reflection somewhat
akin, with others besides. In his several
calls at the Court his reception has been
both welcome and warm. Still, not beyond
the bounds of well-bred hospitality. But
why on each and every occasion has he
found a gentleman there—the same every
time—George Shenstone by name? There
before him, and staying after! And this

very day, what meant Mr. Shenstone by
that sudden and abrupt departure? Above
all, why her distraught look, with the sigh
accompanying it, as the baronet's son went
galloping out of the gate? Having seen
the one, and heard the other, Captain
Ryecroft has misinterpreted both. No
wonder his reluctance to speak words of
love.

And so for a time they are silent, the
dread of misconception, with consequent
fear of committal, holding their lips sealed.
On a simple utterance now may hinge their
life's happiness, or its misery.

Nor is it so strange, that in a moment
fraught with such mighty consequence, conversation should be not only timid, but
commonplace. They who talk of love's
eloquence, but think of it in its lighter
phases—perhaps its lying. When truly,
deeply, felt it is dumb, as devout worshipper
in the presence of the divinity worshipped.
Here, side by side, are two highly organized
beings—a man handsome and courageous,
a woman beautiful and aught but timid—

both well up in the accomplishments, and gifted with the graces of life—loving each other to their souls' innermost depths, yet embarrassed in manner, and constrained in speech, as though they were a couple of rustics! More; for Corydon would fling his arms around his Phyllis, and give her an eloquent smack, which she with like readiness would return.

Very different the behaviour of these in the pavilion. They stand for a time silent as statues—though not without a tremulous motion, scarce perceptible—as if the amorous electricity around stifled their breathing, for the time hindering speech. And when at length this comes, it is of no more significance than what might be expected between two persons lately introduced, and feeling but the ordinary interest in one another!

It is the lady who speaks first :—

" I understand you've been but a short while resident in our neighbourhood, Captain Ryecroft ? "

" Not quite three months, Miss Wynn.

Only a week or two before I had the pleasure
of making your acquaintance."

"Thank you for calling it a pleasure.
Not much in the manner, I should say;
but altogether the contrary," she laughs,
adding—

"And how do you like our Wye?"

"Who could help liking it?"

"There's been much said of its scenery
—in books and newspapers. You really
admire it?"

"I do, indeed." His preference is pardonable under the circumstances. "I think
it the finest in the world."

"What! you such a great traveller! In
the tropics too; upon rivers that run between
groves of evergreen trees, and over sands of
gold! Do you really mean that, Captain
Ryecroft?"

"Really—truthfully. Why not, Miss
Wynn?"

"Because I supposed those grand rivers
we read of were all so much superior to our
little Herefordshire stream; in flow of
water, scenery, everything——"

"Nay, not everything!" he says, interruptingly. "In volume of water they may be; but far from it in other respects. In some it is superior to them all—Rhine, Rhone, ah! Hippocrene itself!"

His tongue is at length getting loosed.

"What other respects?" she asks.

"The forms reflected in it," he answers hesitatingly.

"Not those of vegetation! Surely our oaks, elms, and poplars cannot be compared with the tall palms and graceful tree ferns of the tropics?"

"No; not those."

"Our buildings neither, if photography tells truth, which it should. Those wonderful structures—towers, temples, pagodas —of which it has given us the *fac similes*— far excel anything we have on the Wye—or anything in England. Even our Tintern, which we think so very grand, were but as nothing to them. Isn't that so?"

"True," he says, assentingly. "One must admit the superiority of Oriental architecture."

" But you've not told me what form our English river reflects, so much to your admiration !"

He has a fine opportunity for poetical reply. The image is in his mind—her own—with the word upon his tongue, "woman's." But he shrinks from giving it utterance. Instead, retreating from the position he had assumed, he rejoins evasively :—

" The truth is, Miss Wynn, I've had a surfeit of tropical scenery, and was only too glad once more to feast my eyes on the hill and dale landscapes of dear old England. I know none to compare with these of the Wyeside."

" It's very pleasing to hear you say that—to me especially. It's but natural I should love our beautiful Wye—I, born on its banks, brought up on them, and, I suppose, likely to——"

" What?" he asks, observing that she has paused in her speech.

" Be buried on them !" she answers, laughingly. She intended to have said " Stay on them for the rest of my life."

" You'll think that a very grave conclusion," she adds, keeping up the laugh.

" One at all events very far off—it is to be hoped. An eventuality not to arise, till after you've passed many long and happy days — whether on the Wye, or elsewhere."

"Ah! who can tell? The future is a sealed book to all of us."

" Yours need not be—at least as regards its happiness. I think that is assured."

" Why do you say so, Captain Ryecroft ?"

" Because it seems to me, as though you had yourself the making of it."

He is saying no more than he thinks; far less. For he believes she could make fate itself—control it, as she can his. And as he would now confess to her—is almost on the eve of it—but hindered by recalling that strange look and sigh sent after Shenstone. His fond fancies, the sweet dreams he has been indulging in ever since making her acquaintance, may have been but illusions. She may be playing with him, as he would with a fish on his hook. As yet, no

word of love has passed her lips.   Is there
thought of it in her heart—for him?

"In what way?   What mean you?" she
asks, her liquid eyes turned upon him with
a look of searching interrogation.

The question staggers him.   He does not
answer it as he would, and again replies
evasively—somewhat confusedly.

"Oh! I only meant, Miss Wynn—that
you so young—so—well, with all the world
before you—surely have your happiness in
your own hands."

If he knew how much it is in his he
would speak more courageously, and possibly
with greater plainness.   But he knows not,
nor does she tell him.   She, too, is cautiously
retentive, and refrains taking advantage of
his words, full of suggestion.

It will need another *seance*—possibly more
than one—before the real confidence can be
exchanged between them.   Natures like
theirs do not rush into confession as the
common kind.   With them it is as with
the wooing of eagles.

She simply rejoins:

" I wish it were," adding with a sigh, " Far from it, I fear."

He feels as if he had drifted into a dilemma—brought about by his own *gaucherie* —from which something seen up the river, on the opposite side, offers an opportunity to escape—a house. It is the quaint old habitation of Tudor times. Pointing to it, he says:

" A very odd building, that! If I've been rightly informed, Miss Wynn, it belongs to a relative of yours?"

" I have a cousin who lives there."

The shadow suddenly darkening her brow, with the slightly explicit rejoinder, tells him he is again on dangerous ground. He attributes it to the character he has heard of Mr. Murdock. His cousin is evidently disinclined to converse about him.

And she is; the shadow still staying. If she knew what is at that moment passing within Glyngog—could but hear the conversation carried on at its dining table —it might be darker. It is dark enough in her heart, as on her face—possibly from a presentiment.

Ryecroft more than ever embarrassed, feels it a relief when Ellen Lees, with the Rev. Mr. Musgrave as her cavalier attendant—they, too, straying solitarily—approach near enough to be hailed, and invited into the pavilion.

So the dialogue between the cautious lovers comes to an end—to both of them unsatisfactory enough. For this day their love must remain unrevealed ; though never man and woman more longed to learn the sweet secret of each other's heart.

CHAPTER XV.

WHILE the sports are in progress outside
Llangorren Court, inside Glyngog House
is being eaten that dinner to commence
with salmon in season and end with pheasant out.

It is early; but the Murdocks, often glad
to eat what Americans call a " square meal,"
have no set hours for eating, while the priest
is not particular.

In the faces of the trio seated at the
table, a physiognomist might find interesting study, and note expressions that
would puzzle Lavater himself. Nor could
they be interpreted by the conversation
which, at first, only refers to topics of a
trivial nature. But now and then, a *mot* of
double meaning let down by Rogier, and a
glance surreptitiously exchanged between

him and his countryman, tell that the thoughts of these two are running upon themes different from those about which are their words.

Murdock, by no means of a trusting disposition, but ofttimes furiously jealous—has nevertheless, in this respect, no suspicion of the priest, less from confidence than a sort of contempt for the pallid puny creature, whom he feels he could crush in a moment of mad anger. And broken though he be, the stalwart, and once strong, Englishman could still do that. To imagine such a man as Rogier a rival in the affections of his own wife, would be to be little himself. Besides, he holds fast to that proverbial faith in the spiritual adviser, not always well founded—in his case certainly misplaced. Knowing nought of this, however, their exchanged looks, however markedly significant, escape his observation. Even if he did observe, he could not read in them aught relating to love. For, this day there is not; the thoughts of both are absorbed by a different passion—cupidity. They are bent upon a scheme of no common magnitude, but grand and comprehensive—neither more nor less than to get possession of an estate worth £10,000 a year—that Llangorren. They know its value as well as the steward who gives receipts for its rents.

It is no new notion with them; but one for some time entertained, and steps considered. Still nothing definite either conceived, or determined on. A task, so herculean, as dangerous and difficult, will need care in its conception, and time for its execution. True, it might be accomplished, almost instantaneously with six inches of steel, or as many drops of belladonna. Nor would two of the three seated at the table stick at employing such means. Olympe Renault, and Gregoire Rogier have entertained thoughts of them—if not more. In the third is the obstructor. Lewin Murdock would cheat at dice and cards, do money-lenders without remorse, and tradesmen without mercy, ay, steal, if occasion offered; but murder—that is different—being a crime not only unpleasant to contemplate, but perilous to commit. He would be willing to rob Gwendoline Wynn of her property—glad to do it—if he only knew how—but to take away her life, he is not yet up to that.

But he is drawing up to it, urged by desperate circumstances, and spurred on by his wife, who loses no opportunity of bewailing their broken fortunes, and reproaching him for them; at her back the Jesuit secretly instructing, and dictating.

Not till this day have they found him in the mood for being made more familiar with their design. Whatever his own disposition, his ear has been hitherto deaf to their hints, timidly, and ambiguously given. But to-day things appear more promising, as evinced by his angry exclamation " Never ! " Hence their delight at hearing it.

During the earlier stages of the dinner, as already said, they converse about ordinary subjects, like the lovers in the pavilion, silent upon that paramount in their minds. How different the themes—as love itself

from murder ! And just as the first word
was unspoken in the summer-house at
Llangorren, so is the last unheard in the
dining-room of Glyngog.

While the blotcher is being carved with
a spoon—there is no fish slice among the
chattels of Mr. Murdock—the priest in
good appetite, and high glee, pronounces it
" crimp." He speaks English like a native,
and is even up in its provincialisms; few
in Herefordshire whose dialect is of the
purest.

The phrase of the fishmonger received
smilingly, the salmon is distributed and
handed across the table; the attendance of
the slavey, with claws not over clean, and
ears that might be unpleasantly sharp, having been dispensed with.

There is wine without stint; for although
Murdock's town tradesmen may be hard of
heart, in the Welsh Harp there is a tender
string he can still play upon; the Boniface
of the Rugg's Ferry hostelry having a belief
in his *post obit* expectations. Not such an
indifferent wine either, but some of the

choicest vintage. The guests of the Harp, however rough in external appearance and rude in behaviour—have wonderfully refined ideas about drink, and may be often heard calling for "fizz"—some of them as well acquainted with the qualities of Möet and Cliquot, as a connoisseur of the most fashionable club.

Profiting by their æsthetic tastes, Lewin Murdock is enabled to set wines upon his table of the choicest brands. Light Bordeaux first with the fish, then sherry with the heavier greens and bacon, followed by champagne as they get engaged upon the pheasant.

At this point the conversation approaches a topic, hitherto held in reserve, Murdock himself starting it:—

"So, my cousin Gwen's going to get married, eh! are you sure of that, Father Rogier?"

"I wish I were as sure of going to heaven."

"But what sort of man is he? you haven't told us."

" Yes, I have. You forget my description, Monsieur—cross between Mars and Phœbus—strength herculean ; sure to be father to a progeny numerous as that which spring from the head of Medusa—enough of them to make heirs for Llangorren to the end of time—keep you out of the property if you lived to be the age of Methuselah. Ah ! a fine-looking fellow, I can assure you ; against whom the baronet's son, with his rubicund cheeks and hay-coloured hair, wouldn't stand the slightest chance—even were there nothing more to recommend the martial stranger. But there is."

" What more ? "

" The mode of his introduction to the lady—that quite romantic."

" How was he introduced ?"

" Well, he made her acquaintance on the water. It appears Mademoiselle Wynn and her companion Lees, were out on the river for a row alone. Unusual that ! Thus out, some fellows—Forest of Dean dwellers— offered them insult ; from which a gentleman angler, who chanced to be whipping the stream close by, saved them—he no other than *le Capitaine Ryecroft*. With such commencement of acquaintance, a man couldn't be much worth, who didn't know how to improve it—even to terminating in marriage if he wished. And with such a rich heiress as Mademoiselle Gwendoline Wynn—to say nought of her personal charms—there are few men who wouldn't wish it so to end. That he, the Hussar officer, captain, colonel, or whatever his rank, does, I've good reason to believe, as also that he will succeed in accomplishing his desires ; no more doubt of it than of my being seated at this table. Yes ; sure as I sit here that man will be the master of Llangorren."

" I suppose he will ; " " must," rejoins Murdock, drawing out the words as though not greatly concerned, one way, or the other.

Olympe looks dissatisfied, but not Rogier nor she, after a glance from the priest, which seems to say " Wait." He himself intends waiting till the drink has done its work.

Taking the hint she remains silent, her

countenance showing calm, as with the con-
tent of innocence, while in her heart is the
guilt of hell, and the deceit of the devil.

She preserves her composure all through,
and soon as the last course is ended, with a
show of dessert placed upon the table—poor
and *pro forma*—obedient to a look from
Rogier, with a slight nod in the direction
of the door, she makes her *congè*, and retires.

Murdock lights his meerschaum, the priest
one of his paper cigarettes—of which he
carries a case—and for some time they sit
smoking and drinking; talking, too, but
upon matters with no relation to that uppermost in their minds. They seem to fear
touching it, as though it were a thing to
contaminate. It is only after repeatedly
emptying their glasses, their courage comes
up to the standard required; that of the
Frenchman first; who, nevertheless, approaches the delicate subject with cautious
circumlocution.

"By the way, M'sieu," he says, "we've
forgotten what we were conversing about,
when summoned to dinner—a meal I've

greatly enjoyed—notwithstanding your de-
preciation of the *menu*. Indeed, a very
bonne bouche your English bacon, and the
greens excellent, as also the *pommes de
terre*. You were speaking of some event,
or circumstance, to be conditional on
your death. What is it? Not the deluge,
I hope! True, your Wye is subject to
sudden floods; might it have ought to do
with them?"

"Why should it?" asks Murdock, not
comprehending the drift.

"Because people sometimes get drowned
in these inundations; indeed, often. Scarce
a week passes without some one falling into
the river, and there remaining, at least till
life is extinct. What with its whirls and
rapids, it's a very dangerous stream. I
wonder at Mademoiselle Wynne venturing
so courageously—so *carelessly* upon it."

The peculiar intonation of the last speech,
with emphasis on the word carelessly, gives
Murdock a glimpse of what it is intended
to point to.

"She's got courage enough," he rejoins,

without appearing to comprehend. "About her carelessness, I don't know."

"But the young lady certainly is careless—recklessly so. That affair of her going out alone is proof of it. What followed may make her more cautious; still, boating is a perilous occupation, and boats, whether for pleasure or otherwise, are awkward things to manage—fickle and capricious as women themselves. Suppose hers should some day go to the bottom she being in it?"

"That would be bad."

"Of course it would. Though, Monsieur Murdock, many men situated as you, instead of grieving over such an accident, would but rejoice at it."

"No doubt they would. But what's the use of talking of a thing not likely to happen?"

"Oh, true! Still, boat accidents being of such common occurrence, one is as likely to befall Mademoiselle Wynn as anybody else. A pity if it should—a misfortune! But so is the other thing."

" What other thing?"

" That such a property as Llangorren should be in the hands of heretics, having but a lame title too. If what I've heard be true, you yourself have as much right to it as your cousin. It were better it belonged to a true son of the Church, as I know you to be, M'sieu."

Murdock receives the compliment with a grimace. He is no hypocrite; still with all his depravity he has a sort of respect for religion, or rather its outward forms—regularly attends Rogier's chapel, and goes through all the ceremonies and genuflexions, just as the Italian bandit after cutting a throat will drop on his knees and repeat a *paternoster* at hearing the distant bell of the Angelus.

" A very poor one," he replies, with a half smile, half grin.

" In a worldly sense, you mean? I'm aware, you're not very rich."

" In more senses than that. Your Reverence, I've been a great sinner, I admit."

" Admission is a good sign—giving promise of repentance, which need never come too late if a man be disposed to it. It is a deep sin the Church cannot condone—a dark crime indeed."

" Oh, I haven't done anything deserving the name. Only such as a great many others."

" But you might be tempted some day. Whether or not it's my duty, as your spiritual adviser, to point out the true doctrine—how the Vatican views such things. It's after all only a question of balance between good and evil; that is, how much evil a man may have done, and the amount of good he may do. This world is a ceaseless war between God and the devil; and those who wage it in the cause of the former have often to employ the weapons of the latter. In our service the end justifies the means, even though these be what the world calls criminal—ay, even to the TAKING OF LIFE, else why should the great and good Loyola have counselled drawing the sword, himself using it ? "

" True," grunts Murdock, smoking hard,

"you're a great theologian, Father Rogier.
I confess ignorance in such matters; still,
I see reason in what you say."

"You may see it clearer if I set the
application before you. As for instance, if
a man have the right to a certain property,
or estate, and is kept out of it by a quibble,
any steps he might take to possess himself
would be justifiable providing he devote a
portion of his gains to the good cause—
that is, upholding the true faith, and so
benefiting humanity at large. Such an
act is held by the best of our Church
authorities to compensate for any sin committed—supposing the money donation
sufficient to make the amount of good it
may do preponderate over the evil. And
such a man would not only merit absolution, but freely receive it. Now, Monsieur,
do you comprehend me?"

"Quite," says Murdock, taking the pipe
from his mouth and gulping down a half
tumbler of brandy—for he has dropped the
wine. Withal, he trembles at the programme thus metaphorically put before

him, and fears admitting the application to himself.

Soon the more potent spirit takes away his last remnant of timidity, which the tempter perceiving, says:—

"You say you have sinned, Monsieur. And if it were only for that you ought to make amends."

"In what way could I?"

"The way I've been speaking of. Bestow upon the Church the means of doing good, and so deserve indulgence."

"Ah! where am I to find this means?"

"On the other side of the river."

"You forget that there's more than the stream between."

"Not much to a man who would be true to himself."

"I'm that man all over." The brandy has made him bold, at length untying his tongue, while unsteadying it. "Yes, Père Rogier; I'm ready for anything that will release me from this damnable fix—debt over the ears—duns every day. Ha! I'd be true to myself, never fear!"

"It needs being true to the Church as well."

"I'm willing to be that when I have the chance, if ever I have it. And to get it I'd risk life. Not much if I lose it. It's become a burden to me, heavier than I can bear."

"You may make it as light as a feather, M'sieu; cheerful as that of any of those gay gentry you saw disporting themselves on the lawn at Llangorren—even that of its young mistress."

"How, *Père ?* "

"By yourself becoming its master"

"Ah! if I could."

"You can!"

"With safety?"

"Perfect safety."

"And without committing"—he fears to speak the ugly English word, but expresses the idea in French—"*cette dernier coup ?* "

"Certainly! Who dreams of that? Not I, M'sieu."

"But how is it to be avoided?"

" Easily."

" Tell me, Father Rogier ! "

" Not to-night, Murdock ! " — he has dropped the distant M'sieu—" Not to-night. It's a matter that calls for reflection — consideration, calm and careful. Time, too. Ten thousand *livrés esterlies* per annum ! We must both ponder upon it—sleep nights, and think days, over it— possibly have to draw Coracle Dick into our deliberations. But not to-night— *Pardieu!* it's ten o'clock ! And I have business to do before going to bed. I must be off."

" No, your Reverence ; not till you've had another glass of wine."

" One more then. But let me take it standing—the *tasse d'estrope*, as you call it."

Murdock assents; and the two rise up to drink the stirrup cup. But only the Frenchman keeps his feet till the glasses are emptied; the other, now dead drunk, dropping back into his chair.

" *Bon soir, Monsieur !* " says the priest,

slipping out of the room, his host answering only by a snore.

For all, Father Rogier does not
leave the house so unceremoniously. In
the porch outside he takes more formal
leave of a woman he there finds waiting
for him. As he joins her going out, she
asks, *sotto voce* :—

" *C'est arrange ?* "

"*Pas encore serait tout suite.*"

This the sole speech that passes between
them; but something besides, which, if
seen by her husband, would cause him to
start from his chair—perhaps some little
sober him.

CHAPTER XVI.

CORACLE DICK.

A TRAVELLER making the tour of the Wye will now and then see moving along its banks, or across the contiguous meadows, what he might take for a gigantic tortoise walking upon its tail ! Mystified by a sight so abnormal, and drawing nigh to get an explanation of it, he will discover that the moving object is after all but a man, carrying a boat upon his back ! Still the tourist will be astonished at a feat so herculean— rival to that of Atlas—and will only be altogether enlightened when the boat-bearer lays down his burden—which, if asked, he will obligingly do—and permits him, the stranger, to satisfy his curiosity by an inspection of it. Set square on the sward at his feet, he will look upon a craft quaint as was ever launched on lake, stream, or tidal wave. For he will be looking at a "coracle."

Not only quaint in construction, but singularly ingenious in design, considering the ends to be accomplished. In addition, historically interesting; so much as to deserve more than passing notice, even in the pages of a novel. Nor will I dismiss it without a word, however it may seem out of place.

In shape the coracle bears resemblance to the half of a humming-top, or Swedish turnip cloven longitudinally, the cleft face scooped out leaving but the rind. The timbers consist of slender saplings—peeled and split to obtain lightness—disposed, some fore and aft, others athwart-ships, still others diagonally, as struts and ties, all having their ends in a band of wickerwork, which runs round the gunwale, holding them firmly in place, itself forming the rail. Over this framework is stretched a covering of tarred, and, of course, waterproof canvas, tight as a drum. In olden times it was the skin of ox or horse, but the modern material

is better, because lighter, and less liable to
decay, besides being cheaper.   There is but
one seat, or thwart, as the coracle is designed for only a single occupant, though
in a pinch it can accommodate two.
This is a thin board, placed nearly amidships, partly supported by the wicker rail,
and in part by another piece of light scant-
ling, set edgeways underneath.

In all things ponderosity is as much as
possible avoided, since one of the essential
purposes of the coracle is " portage ;" and to
facilitate this it is furnished with a leathern
strap, the ends attached near each extremity
of the thwart, to be passed across the breast
when the boat is borne overland.   The
bearer then uses his oar—there is but one,
a broad-bladed paddle—by way of walking-
stick ; and so proceeds, as already said, like
a tortoise travelling on its tail !

In this convenience of carriage lies the
ingenuity of the structure—unique and
clever beyond anything in the way of water-
craft I have observed elsewhere, either
among savage or civilized nations.   The

only thing approaching it in this respect is
the birch bark canoe of the Esquimaux and
the Chippeway Indians. But though more
beautiful this, it is far behind our native
craft in an economic sense—in cheapness
and readiness. For while the Chippewayan
would be stripping his bark from the tree,
and re-arming it—to say nought of fitting
to the frame timbers, stitching, and paying
it—a subject of King Caradoc would have
launched his coracle upon the Wye, and
paddled it from Plinlimmon to Chepstow;
as many a modern Welshman would the
same.

Above all, is the coracle of rare historic
interest—as the first venture upon water of
a people—the ancestors of a nation that now
rules the sea—their descendants proudly
styling themselves its "Lords"—not without right and reason.

Why called "coracle" is a matter of
doubt and dispute; by most admitted as a
derivative from the Latin *corum*—a skin;
this being its original covering. But certainly a misconception; since we have

P 2

historic evidence of the basket and hide boat
being in use around the shores of Albion
hundreds of years before these ever saw
Roman ship or standard. Besides, at the
same early period, under the almost
homonym of "corragh," it floated—still
floats—on the waters of the Lerne, far
west of anywhere the Romans ever went.
Among the common people on the Wye
it bears a less ancient appellation—that of
"truckle."

From whatever source the craft derives
its name, it has itself given a sobriquet to
one of the characters of our tale—Richard
Dempsey. Why the poacher is thus distinguished it is not easy to tell; possibly
because he, more than any other in his
neighbourhood, makes use of it, and is often
seen trudging about the river bottoms with
the huge carapace on his shoulders. It serves
his purpose better than any other kind of
boat, for Dick, though a snarer of hares and
pheasants, is more of a salmon poacher, and
for this—the water branch of his amphibious calling—the coracle has a special

adaptation. It can be lifted out of the river, or launched upon it anywhere, without leaving trace; whereas with an ordinary skiff the moorings might be marked, the embarkation observed, and the night netter followed to his netting-place by the watchful water bailiff.

Despite his cunning and the handiness of his craft, Dick has not always come off scot-free. His name has several times figured in the reports of Quarter Sessions, and himself in the cells of the county gaol. This only for poaching; but he has also served a spell in prison for crime of a less venal kind—burglary. As the "job" was done in a distant shire, there has been nothing heard of it in that where he now resides. The worst known of him in the neighbourhood is his game and fish trespassing, though there is worse suspected. He whose suspicions are strongest being the waterman, Wingate.

But Jack may be wronging him, for a certain reason—the most powerful that ever swayed the passion or warped the judgment of man—rivalry for the affections of a woman.

No heart, however hardened, is proof against the shafts of Cupid; and one has penetrated the heart of Coracle Dick, as deeply as has another that of Jack Wingate. And both from the same bow and quiver— the eyes of Mary Morgan.

She is the daughter of a small farmer who lives by the Wyeside; and being a farmer's daughter, above both in social rank, still not so high but that Love's ladder may reach her, and each lives in hope he may some day scale it. For Evan Morgan holds as a tenant, and his land is of limited acreage. Dick Dempsey and Jack Wingate are not the only ones who wish to have him for a father-in-law, but the two most earnest, and whose chances seem best. Not that these are at all equal; on the contrary, greatly disproportionate, Dick having the advantage. In his favour is the fact that Farmer Morgan is a Roman Catholic—his wife fanatically so —he, Dempsey, professing the same faith;

while Wingate is a Protestant of pronounced type.

Under these circumstances Coracle has a
friend at head-quarters, in Mrs. Morgan,
and an advocate who visits there, in the
person of Father Rogier.

With this united influence in his favour,
the odds against the young waterman are
great, and his chances might appear slight
—indeed would be, were it not for an influence to counteract. He, too, has a partisan
inside the citadel, and a powerful one; since
it is the girl herself. He knows—is sure
of it, as man may be of any truth, com-
municated to him by loving lips amidst
showers of kisses. For all this has passed
between Mary Morgan and himself.

And nothing of it between her and
Richard Dempsey. Instead, on her part,
coldness and distant reserve. It would be
disdain—ay, scorn — if she dare show it;
for she hates the very sight of the man.
But, controlled and close watched, she has
learnt to smile when she would frown.

The world—or that narrow circle of it

immediately surrounding and acquainted with the Morgan family—wonders at the favourable reception it vouchsafes to Richard Dempsey—a known and noted poacher.

But in justice to Mrs. Morgan it should be said, she has but slight acquaintance with the character of the man—only knows it as represented by Rogier. Absorbed in her paternosters, she gives little heed to ought else; her thoughts, as her actions, being all of the dictation, and under the direction, of the priest. In her eyes Coracle Dick is as the latter has painted him, thus—

"A worthy fellow—poor it is true, but honest withal; a little addicted to fish and game taking, as many another good man. Who wouldn't with such laws—unrighteous —oppressive to the poor? Were they otherwise, the poacher would be a patriot. As for Dempsey, they who speak ill of him are only the envious—envying his good looks, and fine mental qualities. For he's clever, and they can't say nay—energetic, and likely to make his way in the world.

Yet, one thing he would make—that's a good husband to your daughter Mary—one who has the strength and courage to take care of her."

So counsels the priest; and as he can make Mrs. Morgan believe black white, she is ready to comply with his counsel. If the result rested on her, Coracle Dick would have nothing to fear.

But it does not—he knows it does not— and is troubled. With all the influence in his favour, he fears that other influence against him—if against him, far more than a counterpoise to Mrs. Morgan's religious predilections, or the partisanship of his priest. Still he is not sure; one day the slave of sweet confidence, the next a prey to black bitter jealousy. And thus he goes on doting and doubting, as if he were never to know the truth.

A day comes when he is made acquainted with it, or, rather, a night; for it is after sundown the revelation reaches him — indeed, nigh on to midnight. His favoured, yet defeated, aspirations, are more than

twelve months old. They have been active
all through the preceding winter, spring,
and summer. It is now autumn; the leaves
are beginning to turn sere, and the last
sheaves have been gathered to the stack.

No shire than that of Hereford more addicted to the joys of the Harvest Home;
this often celebrated in a public and general
way, instead of at the private and particular
farm-house. One such is given upon the
summit of Garran Hill—a grand gathering,
to which all go of the class who attend
such assemblages—small farmers with their
families, their servants too, male and female.
There is a cromlech on the hill's top, around
which they annually congregate, and beside
this ancient relic are set up the symbols
of a more modern time—the Maypole—
though it is Autumn—with its strings and
garlands; the show booths and the refresh-
ment tents, with their display of cakes,
fruits, perry, and cider. And there are
sports of various kinds, pitching the stone,
climbing the greased pole—that of May
now so slippery—jumping, racing in sacks,

dancing—among other dances the Morris—
with a grand *finale* of fireworks.

At this year's fête Farmer Morgan is present, accompanied by his wife and daughter.
It need not be said that Dick Dempsey and
Jack Wingate are there too. They are, and
have been all the afternoon—ever since the
gathering began. But during the hours of
daylight neither approaches the fair creature
to which his thoughts tend, and on which
his eyes are almost constantly turning.
The poacher is restrained by a sense of his
own unworthiness—a knowledge that there
is not the place to make show of his aspirations to one all believe so much above
him ; while the waterman is kept back and
aloof by the presence of the watchful
mother.

With all her watchfulness he finds opportunity to exchange speech with the daughter—only a few words, but enough to make
hell in the heart of Dick Dempsey, who
overhears them.

It is at the closing scene of the spectacle,
when the pyrotechnists are about to send

up their final *feu de joie*, Mrs. Morgan, treated by numerous acquaintances to aniseed and other toothsome drinks, has grown less thoughtful of her charge, which gives Jack Wingate the opportunity he has all along been looking for. Sidling up to the girl, he asks in a tone which tells of lovers *en rapport*, mutually, unmistakably—

" When, Mary ? "

" Saturday night next. The priest's coming to supper. I'll make an errand to the shop, soon as it gets dark."

" Where ? "

" The old place under the big elm."

" You're sure you'll be able ? "

" Sure, never fear, I'll find a way."

" God bless you, dear girl. I'll be there, if anywhere on earth."

This is all that passes between them. But enough—more than enough—for Richard Dempsey. As a rocket, just then going up, throws its glare over his face, as also the others, no greater contrast could be seen or imagined. On the countenances of the lovers an expression of contentment, sweet

and serene ; on his a look such as Mephis-
topheles gave to Gretchen escaping from
his toils.

The curse in Coracle's heart is but hindered from rising to his lips by a fear of its
foiling the vengeance he there and then
determines on.

CHAPTER XVII.

THE "CORPSE CANDLE."

JACK WINGATE lives in a little cottage whose bit of garden ground "brinks" the country road where the latter trends close to the Wye at one of its sharpest sinuosities. The cottage is on the convex side of the bend, having the river at back, with a deep drain, or wash, running up almost to its walls, and forming a fence to one side of the garden. This gives the waterman another and more needed advantage—a convenient docking place for his boat. There the *Mary*, moored, swings to her painter in safety; and when a rise in the river threatens he is at hand to see she be not swept off. To guard against such catastrophe he will start up from his bed at any hour of the night, having more than one reason to be careful of the boat; for, besides being his *gagne-pain*, it bears the name, by himself given, of her the thought of whom sweetens his toil and makes his labour light. For her he bends industriously to his oar, as though he believed every stroke made and every boat's length gained was bringing him nearer to Mary Morgan. And in a sense so is it, whichever way the boat's head may be turned; the farther he rows her the grander grows that heap of gold he is hoarding up against the day when he hopes to become a Benedict. He has a belief that if he could but display before the eyes of Farmer Morgan sufficient money to take a little farm for himself and stock it, he might then remove all obstacles between him and Mary—mother's objections and sinister and sacerdotal influence included.

He is aware of the difference of rank—that social chasm between—being oft bitterly reminded of it ; but, emboldened by Mary's smiles, he has little fear but that he will yet be able to bridge it.

Favouring the programme thus traced out, there is, fortunately, no great strain on his resources by way of drawback; only the maintaining of his own mother, a frugal dame—thrifty besides—who, instead of adding to the current expenses, rather curtails them by the adroit handling of her needle. It would have been a distaff in the olden days.

Thus helped in his housekeeping, the young waterman is enabled to put away almost every shilling he earns by his oar, and this same summer all through till autumn, which it now is, has been more than usually profitable to him, by reason of his so often having Captain Ryecroft as his fare; for although the Hussar officer no longer goes salmon fishing—he has somehow been spoilt for that—there are other excursions upon which he requires the boat, and as ever generously, even lavishly, pays for it.

From one of these the young waterman has but returned; and, after carefully bestowing the *Mary* at her moorings, stepped inside the cottage. It is Saturday —within one hour of sundown—that same

Saturday spoken of "at the Harvest
Home." But though Jack is just home,
he shows no sign of an intention to stay
there; instead, behaves as if he intended
going out again, though not in his boat.

And he does so intend, for a purpose
unsuspected by his mother, to keep that
appointment, made hurriedly, and in a half
whisper, amid the fracas of the fireworks.

The good dame had already set the table
for tea, ready against his arrival, covered it
with a cloth, snow white of course. The
tea-things superimposed, in addition a
dining plate, knife and fork, these for a
succulent beefsteak heard hissing on the
gridiron almost as soon as the *Mary* made
appearance at the mouth of the wash, and,
soon as the boat was docked, done. It is
now on the table, alongside the teapot; its
savoury odour mingling with the fragrance
of the freshly "drawn" tea, fills the
cottage kitchen with a perfume to delight
the gods.

For all, it gives no gratification to Jack
Wingate the waterman. The appetizing

smell of the meat, and the more ethereal aroma of the Chinese shrub, are alike lost upon him. Appetite he has none, and his thoughts are elsewhere.

Less from observing his abstraction, than the slow, negligent movements of his knife and fork, the mother asks—

"What's the matter with ye, Jack? Ye don't eat!"

"I ain't hungry, mother."

"But ye been out since mornin', and tooked nothing wi' you!"

"True; but you forget who I ha' been out with. The captain ain't the man to let his boatman be a hungered. We war down the day far as Symond's yat, where he treated me to dinner at the hotel. The daintiest kind o' dinner, too. No wonder at my not havin' much care for eatin' now —nice as you've made things, mother."

Notwithstanding the compliment, the old lady is little satisfied—less as she observes the continued abstraction of his manner. He fidgets uneasily in his chair, every now and then giving a glance at the

little Dutch clock suspended against the
wall, which in loud ticking seems to say,
"You'll be late—you'll be late." She
suspects something of the cause, but
inquires nothing of it. Instead, she but
observes, speaking of the patron :—

"He be very good to ye, Jack."

"Ah! that he be; good to every one
as comes nigh o' him—and 's desarvin'
it."

"But ain't he stayin' in the neighbourhood longer than he first spoke of doin'?"

"Maybe he is. Grand gentry such as
he ain't like us poor folk. They can go
and come whens'ever it please 'em. I
suppose he have his reasons for remaining."

"Now, Jack, you know he have, an' I've
heerd something about 'em myself."

"What have you heard, mother?"

"Oh, what! Ye han't been a rowin'
him up and down the river now nigh on
five months without findin' out. An' if
you haven't, others have. It's goin' all
about that he's after a young lady as lives
somewhere below. Tidy girl, they say,

tho' I never seed her myself. Is it so, my son? Say!"

"Well, mother, since you've put it straight at me in that way, I won't deny it to you, tho' I'm in a manner bound to saycrecy wi' others. It be true that the Captain have some notion o' such a lady."

"There be a story, too, o' her bein' nigh drownded an' his saving her out o' a boat. Now, Jack, whose boat could that be if it wa'nt your'n?"

"'Twor mine, mother; that's true enough. I would a told you long ago, but he asked me not to talk o' the thing. Besides, I didn't suppose you'd care to hear about it."

"Well," she says, satisfied, "tan't much to me, nor you neyther, Jack; only as the Captain being so kind, we'd both like to know the best about him. If he have took a fancy for the young lady, I hope she return it. She ought after his doin' what he did for her. I han't heerd her name; what be it?"

"She's a Miss Wynn, mother. A very

rich heiress. 'Deed I b'lieve she ain't a
heiress any longer, or won't be, after next
Thursday, sin' that day she comes o' age. An'
that night there's to be a big party at her
place, dancin' an' all sorts o' festivities. I
know it because the Captain's goin' there,
an' has bespoke the boat to take him."

"Wynn, eh? That be a Welsh name.
Wonder if she's any kin o' the great Sir
Watkin."

"Can't say, mother. I believe there be
several branches o' the Wynn family."

"Yes, and all o' the good sort. If she
be one o' the Welsh Wynns, the Captain
can't go far astray in having her for his
wife."

Mrs. Wingate is herself of Cymric ancestry, originally from the shire of Pembroke,
but married to a man of Montgomery,
where Jack was born. It is only of late,
in her widowhood, she has become a resident of Herefordshire.

"So you think he have a notion o' her,
Jack?"

"More'n that, mother. I may as well

tell ye; he be dead in love wi' her. An'
if you seed the young lady herself, ye
wouldn't wonder at it. She be most as
good-looking as——"

Jack suddenly interrupted himself on
the edge of a revelation he would rather
not make, to his mother nor any one else.
For he has hitherto been as careful in keeping his own secret as that of his patron.

"As who?" she asks, looking him
straight in the face, and with an expression
in her eyes of no common interest—that of
maternal solicitude.

"Who?—well—" he answers confusedly;
"I wor goin' to mention the name o' a girl
who the people 'bout here think the best-
lookin' o' any in the neighbourhood——"

"An' nobody more'n yourself, my son.
You needn't gi'e her name. I know it."

"Oh, mother! what d'ye mean?" he
stammers out, with eyes on the but half-
eaten beefsteak. "I take it they've
been tellin' ye some stories 'bout me."

"No, they han't. Nobody's sayed a
word about ye relatin' to that. I've seed

it for myself, long since, though you've tried
hide it. I'm not goin' to blame ye eyther,
for I believe she be a tidy proper girl. But
she's far aboon you, my son; and ye maun
mind how you behave yourself. If the
young lady be anythin' like's good-lookin'
as Mary Morgan——"

"Yes, mother! that's the strangest
thing o' all——"

He interrupts her, speaking excitedly;
again interrupting himself.

"What's strangest?" she inquires with
a look of wonderment.

"Never mind, mother! I'll tell you all
about it some other time. I can't now;
you see it's nigh nine o' the clock."

"Well; an' what if't be?"

"Because I may be too late."

"Too late for what? Surely you arn't
goin' out again the night?" She asks this,
seeing him rise up from his chair.

"I must, mother."

"But why?"

"Well, the boat's painter's got frailed,
and I want a bit o' whipcord to lap it with.

They have the thing at the Ferry shop, and I must get there afores they shut up."

A fib, perhaps pardonable, as the thing he designs lapping is not his boat's painter, but the waist of Mary Morgan, and not with slender whipcord, but his own stout arms.

"Why won't it do in the mornin'?" asks the ill-satisfied mother.

"Well, ye see, there's no knowin' but that somebody may come after the boat. The Captain mayent, but he may, changin' his mind. Anyhow, he'll want her to go down to them grand doin's at Llangowen Court?"

"Llangowen Court?"

"Yes; that's where the young lady lives."

"That's to be on Thursday, ye sayed?"

"True; but, then, there may come a fare the morrow, an' what if there do? 'Tain't the painter only as wants splicin', there's a bit o' a leak sprung close to the cutwater, an' I must hae some pitch to pay it."

If Jack's mother would only step out,

and down to the ditch where the *Mary* is
moored, with a look at the boat, she would
make him out a liar. Its painter is smooth
and clean as a piece of gimp, not a strand
unravelled—while but two or three gallons
of bilge water at the boat's bottom attest
to there being little or no leakage.

But she, good dame, is not thus suspicious,
instead so reliant on her son's truthfulness,
that, without questioning further, she con-
sents to his going, only with a proviso
against his staying, thus appealingly put—

"Ye won't be gone long, my son! I
know ye won't!"

"Indeed I shan't, mother. But why be
you so partic'lar about my goin' out—this
night more'n any other?"

"Because, Jack, this day, more'n most
others, I've been feelin' bothered like, and
a bit frightened."

"Frightened o' what? There han't
been nobody to the house—has there?"

"No; ne'er a rover since you left me in
the mornin'."

"Then what's been a scarin' ye, mother?"

" 'Deed, I don't know, unless it ha' been brought on by the dream I had last night. 'Twer' a dreadful unpleasant one. I didn't tell you o' it 'fore ye went out, thinkin' it might worry ye."

" Tell me now, mother."

" It hadn't nought to do wi' us ourselves, after all. Only concernin' them as live nearest us."

" Ha ! the Morgans ? "

" Yes ; the Morgans."

" Oh, mother, what did you dream about them ?"

"That I wor standin' on the big hill above their house, in the middle o' the night, wi' black darkness all round me ; and there lookin' down what should I see comin' out o' their door ?"

" What ?"

" The canwyll corph ! "

" The canwyll corph ?"

" Yes, my son ; I seed it—that is I dreamed I seed it—coming just out o' the farm-house door, then through the yard, and over the foot-plank at the bottom o'

the orchard, when it went flarin' up the
meadows straight towards the ferry.
Though ye can't see that from the hill, I
dreamed I did ; an' seed the candle go on
to the chapel an' into the buryin' ground.
That woked me."

" What nonsense, mother ! A ridiklous
superstition ! I thought you'd left all that
sort o' stuff behind, in the mountains o'
Montgomery, or Pembrokeshire, where the
thing comes from, as I've heerd you say."

" No, my son ; it's not stuff, nor superstition neyther ; though English people say
that to put slur upon us Welsh. Your
father before ye believed in the *Canwyll
Corph*, and wi' more reason ought I, your
mother. I never told you, Jack, but the
night before your father died I seed it go
past our own door, and on to the graveyard
o' the church where he now lies. Sure as
we stand here there be some one doomed in
the house o' Evan Morgan. There be only
three in the family. I do hope it an't her
as ye might some day be wantin' me to
call daughter."

"Mother! You'll drive me mad! I tell ye it's all nonsense. Mary Morgan be at this moment healthy and strong—most as much as myself. If the dead 'candle ye've been dreamin' about we're all o' it true, it couldn't be a burnin' for her. More like for Mrs. Morgan, who's half daft by believing in church candles and such things —enough to turn her crazy, if it doesn't kill her outright. As for you, my dear mother, don't let the dream bother you the least bit. An' ye mustn't be feeling lonely, as I shan't be long gone. I'll be back by ten sure."

Saying which, he sets his straw hat jauntily on his thick curly hair, gives his guernsey a straightening twitch, and, with a last cheering look and encouraging word to his mother, steps out into the night.

Left alone, she feels lonely withal, and more than ever afraid. Instead of sitting down to her needle, or making to remove the tea-things, she goes to the door, and there stays, standing on its threshold and peering into the darkness—for it is a pitch

dark night—she sees, or fancies, a light
moving across the meadows, as if it came
from Farmer Morgan's house, and going in
the direction of Rugg's Ferry. While she
continues gazing, it twice crosses the
Wye, by reason of the river's bend.

As no mortal hand could thus carry it,
surely it is the *canwyll corph !*

CHAPTER XVIII.

A CAT IN THE CUPBOARD.

EVAN MORGAN is a tenant-farmer, holding Abergann. By Herefordshire custom, every farm or its stead, has a distinctive appellation. Like the land belonging to Glyngog, that of Abergann lies against the sides of a sloping glen—one of the hundreds or thousands of lateral ravines that run into the valley of the Wye. But, unlike the old manor-house, the domicile of the farmer is at the glen's bottom and near the river's bank; nearer yet to a small influent stream, rapid and brawling, which sweeps past the lower end of the orchard in a channel worn deep into the soft sandstone.

Though with the usual imposing array of enclosure walls, the dwelling itself is not large nor the outbuildings extensive; for the arable acreage is limited. This because the ridges around are too high pitched for ploughing, and if ploughed would be unproductive. They are not even in pasture, but overgrown with woods; less for the sake of the timber, which is only scrub, than as a covert for foxes. They are held in hand by Evan Morgan's landlord—a noted Nimrod.

For the same reason the farm-house stands in a solitary spot, remote from any other dwelling. The nearest is the cottage of the Wingates—distant about half a mile, but neither visible from the other. Nor is there any direct road between, only a footpath, which crosses the brook at the bottom of the orchard, thence running over a wooded ridge to the main highway. The last, after passing close to the cottage, as already said, is deflected away from the river by this same ridge, so that when Evan Morgan would drive anywhere beyond the boundaries of his farm, he must pass out through a long lane, so narrow that were he to meet any one driving in, there would be a deadlock. However, there is no danger; as the only vehicles having occasion to use this thoroughfare are his own farm waggon and a lighter 'trap' in which he goes to market, and occasionally with his wife and daughter to merry-makings.

When the three are in it there is none of his family at home. For he has but one child—a daughter. Nor would he long have her were a half-score of young fellows allowed their way. At least this number would be willing to take her off his hands and give her a home elsewhere. Remote as is the farm-house of Abergann, and narrow the lane leading to it, there are many who would be glad to visit there, if invited.

In truth a fine girl is Mary Morgan, tall, bright haired, and with blooming cheeks, beside which red rose leaves would seem *fade*. Living in a town she would be its talk; in a village its belle. Even from that secluded glen has the fame of her beauty gone forth and afar. Of husbands she could have her choice, and among men much richer than her father.

In her heart she has chosen one, not only much poorer, but lower in social rank—

Jack Wingate. She loves the young water-man, and wants to be his wife; but knows she cannot without the consent of her parents. Not that either has signified opposition, since they have never been asked. Her longings in that direction she has kept secret from them. Nor does she so much dread refusal by the father. Evan Morgan had been himself poor—began life as a farm labourer—and, though now an employer of such, his pride had not kept pace with his prosperity. Instead, he is, as ever, the same modest, unpresuming man, of which the lower middle classes of the English people present many noble examples. From him Jack Wingate would have little to fear on the score of poverty. He is well acquainted with the young waterman's character, knows it to be good, and has observed the efforts he is making to better his condition in life; it may be with suspicion of the motive, at all events, admiringly—remembering his own. And although a Roman Catholic, he is anything but bigoted. Were he the only one to be consulted his daughter might wed with the man upon whom she has fixed her affections, at any time it pleases them—ay, at any place, too, even within the walls of a Protestant Church! By him neither would Jack Wingate be rejected on the score of religion.

Very different with his wife. Of all the worshippers who compose the congregation at the Rugg's Ferry Chapel none bend the knee to Baal as low as she; and over no one does Father Rogier exercise such influence. Baneful it is like to be; since not only has he control of the mother's conduct, but through that may also blight the happiness of the daughter.

Apart from religious fanaticism, Mrs. Morgan is not a bad woman—only a weak one. As her husband, she is of humble birth, and small beginnings; like him, too, neither has prosperity affected her in the sense of worldly ambition. Perhaps better if it had. Instead of spoiling, a little social pride might have been a bar to the dangerous aspirations of Richard

Dempsey—even with the priest standing sponsor for him. But she has none, her whole soul being absorbed by blind devotion to a faith which scruples not at anything that may assist in its propagandism.

* * * * * *

It is the Saturday succeeding the festival of the Harvest Home, a little after sunset, and the priest is expected at Abergann. He is a frequent visitor there; by Mrs. Morgan ever made welcome, and treated to the best cheer the farm-house can afford; plate, knife, and fork always placed for him. And, to do him justice, he may be deemed in a way worthy of such hospitality; for he is, in truth, a most entertaining personage; can converse on any subject, and suit his conversation to the company, whether high or low. As much at home with the wife of the Welsh farmer as with the French *ex-cocotte*, and equally so in the companionship of Dick Dempsey, the poacher. In his hours of *far niente* all are alike to him.

This night he is to take supper at Abergann, and Mrs. Morgan, seated in the farm-

R 2

house parlour, awaits his arrival. A snug little apartment, tastefully furnished, but with a certain air of austerity, observable in Roman Catholic houses; this by reason of some pictures of saints hanging against the walls, an image of the Virgin and, standing niche-like in a corner, one of the Crucifixion over the mantel-shelf, with crosses upon books, and other like symbols.

It is near nine o'clock, and the table is already set out. On grand occasions, as this, the farm-house parlour is transformed into dining or supper room, indifferently. The meal intended to be eaten now is more of the former, differing in there being a tea-tray upon the table, with a full service of cups and saucers, as also in the lateness of the hour. But the odoriferous steam escaping from the kitchen, drifted into the parlour when its door is opened, tells of something in preparation more substantial than a cup of tea, with its usual accompaniment of bread and butter. And there is a fat capon roasting upon the spit, with a frying-pan full of sausages on the dresser, ready to be clapped upon the fire at the proper moment—as soon as the expected guest makes his appearance.

And in addition to the tea-things, there is a decanter of sherry on the table, and will be another of brandy when brought on —Father Rogier's favourite tipple, as Mrs. Morgan has reason to know. There is a full bottle of this—Cognac of best brand —in the larder cupboard, still corked as it came from the "Welsh Harp," where it cost six shillings—The Rugg's Ferry hostelry, as already intimated, dealing in drinks of a rather costly kind. Mary has been directed to draw the cork, decant, and bring the brandy in, and for this purpose has just gone off to the larder. Thence instantly returning, but without either decanter or Cognac! Instead with a tale which sends a thrill of consternation through her mother's heart. The cat has been in the cupboard, and there made havoc—upset the brandy bottle, and sent it rolling off the shelf on the stone flags of the floor! Broken, of course, and the contents—

No need for further explanation, Mrs. Morgan does not seek it. Nor does she stay to reflect on the disaster, but how it may be remedied. It will not mend matters to chastise the cat, nor cry over the spilt brandy, any more than if it were milk.

On short reflection she sees but one way to restore the broken bottle—by sending to the " Welsh Harp " for a whole one.

True, it will cost another six shillings, but she recks not of the expense. She is more troubled about a messenger. Where, and how, is one to be had? The farm labourers have long since left. They are all Benedicts, on board wages, and have departed for their respective wives and homes. There is a cow-boy, yet he is also absent; gone to fetch the kine from a far-off pasturing place, and not be back in time; while the one female domestic maid-of-all-work is busy in the kitchen, up to her ears among pots and pans, her face at a red heat over the range. She could not possibly be spared. " It's very vexatious ! "

exclaims Mrs. Morgan, in a state of lively perplexity.

" It is, indeed!" assents her daughter.

A truthful girl, Mary, in the main; but just now the opposite. For she is not vexed by the occurrence, nor does she deem it a disaster, quite the contrary. And she knows it was no accident, having herself brought it about. It was her own soft fingers, not the cat's claws, that swept that bottle from the shelf, sending it smash upon the stones! Tipped over by no *maladroit* handling of corkscrew, but downright deliberate intention! A stratagem that may enable her to keep the appointment made among the fireworks—that threat when she told Jack Wingate she would "find a way."

Thus is she finding it; and in furtherance she leaves her mother no time to consider longer about a messenger.

" I'll go!" she says, offering herself as one.

The deceit unsuspected, and only the willingness appreciated, Mrs. Morgan rejoins :

"Do! that's a dear girl! It's very good of you, Mary. Here's the money."

While the delighted mother is counting out the shillings, the dutiful daughter whips on her cloak—the night is chilly—and adjusts her hat, the best holiday one, on her head; all the time thinking to herself how cleverly she has done the trick. And with a smile of pardonable deception upon her face, she trips lightly across the threshold, and on through the little flower garden in front.

Outside the gate, at an angle of the enclosure wall, she stops, and stands considering. There are two ways to the Ferry, here forking—the long lane and the shorter footpath. Which is she to take? The path leads down along the side of the orchard; and across the brook by the bridge —only a single plank. This spanning the stream, and originally fixed to the rock at both ends, has of late come loose, and is not safe to be traversed, even by day. At night it is dangerous—still more on one dark as this. And danger of no common kind at any time. The channel through which the streams runs is twenty feet deep, with rough boulders in its bed. One falling from above would at least get broken bones. No fear of that to-night, but something as bad, if not worse. For it has been raining throughout the earlier hours of the day, and there in the brook, now a raging torrent. One dropping into it would be swept on to the river, and there surely drowned, if not before.

It is no dread of any of these dangers which causes Mary Morgan to stand considering which route she will take. She has stepped that plank on nights dark as this, even since it became detached from the fastenings, and is well acquainted with its ways. Were there nought else, she would go straight over it, and along the footpath, which passes the 'big elm.' But it is just because it passes the elm she has now paused and is pondering. Her errand calls for haste, and there she would meet a man sure to delay her. She intends meeting him for all that, and being delayed; but not till on her way back. Considering the darkness and obstructions on the footwalk she may go quicker by the road though roundabout. Returning she can take the path.

This thought in her mind, with, perhaps, remembrance of the adage, 'business before pleasure,' decides her; and drawing closer her cloak, she sets off along the lane.

CHAPTER XIX.

In the shire of Hereford there is no such thing as a village—properly so called. The tourist expecting to come upon one, by the black dot on his guide-book map, will fail to find it. Indeed, he will see only a church with a congregation, not the typical cluster of houses around. But no street, nor rows of cottages, in their midst—the orthodox patch of trodden turf—the "green." Nothing of all that.

Unsatisfied, and inquiring the whereabouts of the village itself, he will get answers, only farther confusing him. One will say "here be it," pointing to no place in particular; a second, "thear," with his eye upon the church; a third, "over yonner," nodding to a shop of miscellaneous wares, also intrusted with the receiving and distributing of letters ; while a fourth, whose ideas run on drink, looks to a house larger than the rest, having a square pictorial signboard, with red lion *rampant*, fox *passant*, horse's head, or such like symbol — proclaiming it an inn, or public.

Not far from, or contiguous to, the church, will be a dwelling-house of special pretension, having a carriage entrance, sweep, and shrubbery of well-grown evergreens—the rectory, or vicarage ; at greater distance, two or three cottages of superior class, by their owners styled " villas," in one of which dwells the doctor, a young Esculapius, just beginning practice, or an old one who has never had much ; in another, the relict of a successful shopkeeper left with an " independence ;" while a third will be occupied by a retired military man—" captain," of course, whatever may have been his rank—possibly a naval officer, or an old salt of the merchant service. In their proper places stand the carpenter's shop and smithy, with their array of reapers, rollers, ploughs, and harrows seeking repair ;

among them perhaps a huge steam-thresh-
ing machine, that has burst its boiler, or
received other damage. Then there are the
houses of the *oi polloi*, mostly labouring
men—their little cottages wide apart, or in
twos and threes together, with no resemblance to the formality of town dwellings,
but quaint in structure, ivy-clad or honey-
suckled, looking and smelling of the country.
Farther along the road is an ancient farm-
stead, its big barns, and other out-buildings,
abutting on the highway, which for some
distance is strewn with a litter of rotting
straw; by its side a muddy pond with ducks
and a half-dozen geese, the gander giving
tongue as the tourist passes by; if a pedestrian with knapsack on his shoulders the
dog barking at him, in the belief he is a
tramp or beggar. Such is the Herefordshire
village, of which many like may be met
along Wyeside.

The collection of houses known as Rugg's
Ferry is in some respects different. It does
not lie on any of the main county thorough-
fares, but a cross-country road ·connecting

the two, that lead along the bounding ridges of the river. That passing through it is but little frequented, as the ferry itself is only for foot passengers, though there is a horse boat which can be had when called for. But the place is in a deep crater-like hollow, where the stream courses between cliffs of the old red sandstone, and can only be approached by the steepest "pitches."

Nevertheless, Rugg's Ferry has its mark upon the Ordnance map, though not with the little crosslet denoting a church. It could boast of no place of worship whatever till Father Rogier laid the foundation of his chapel.

For all, it has once been a brisk place in its days of glory; ere the railroad destroyed the river traffic, and the bargees made it a stopping port, as often the scene of rude, noisy revelry.

It is quieter now, and the tourist passing through might deem it almost deserted. He will see houses of varied construction— thirty or forty of them in all—clinging against the cliff in successive terraces, reached by long rows of steps carved out of the rock; cottages picturesque as Swiss *chalets*, with little gardens on ledges, here and there one trellised with grape vines or other climbers, and a round cone-topped cage of wicker holding captive a jackdaw, magpie, or it may be parrot or starling taught to speak.

Viewing these symbols of innocence, the stranger will imagine himself to have lighted upon a sort of English Arcadia—a fancy soon to be dissipated perhaps by the parrot or starling saluting him with the exclamatory phrases, 'God-damn-ye! go to the devil!—go to the devil!' And while he is pondering on what sort of personage could have instructed the creature in such profanity, he will likely enough see the instructor himself peering out through a partially opened door, his face in startling correspondence with the blasphemous exclamations of the bird. For there are other birds resident at Rugg's Ferry besides those in the cages—several who have themselves been caged in the county g. l. The slightly

altered name bestowed upon the place by
Jack Wingate, as others, is not so inappro-
priate.

It may seem strange such characters con-
gregating in a spot so primitive and rural,
so unlike their customary haunts; incon-
gruous as the ex-belle of Mabille in her
high-heeled *bottines* inhabiting the ancient
manor-house of Glyngog.

But more of an enigma—indeed, a moral,
or psychological puzzle; since one would
suppose it the very last place to find them
in. And yet the explanation may partly lie
in moral and psychological causes. Even
the most hardened rogue has his spells of
sentiment, during which he takes delight in
rusticity; and as the "Ferry" has long
enjoyed the reputation of being a place of
abode for him and his sort, he is there sure
of meeting company congenial. Or the
scent after him may have become too hot in
the town, or city, where he has been dis-
playing his dexterity; while here the
policeman is not a power. The one con-
stable of the district station dislikes tak-

ing, and rather steals through it on his rounds.

Notwithstanding all this, there are some respectable people among its denizens, and many visitors who are gentlemen. Its quaint picturesqueness attracts the tourist; while a stretch of excellent angling ground, above and below, makes it a favourite with amateur fishermen.

Centrally on a platform of level ground, a little back from the river's bank, stands a large three-story house—the village inn— with a swing sign in front, upon which is painted what resembles a triangular grid-iron, though designed to represent a harp. From this the hostelry has its name—the " Welsh Harp ! " But however rough the limning, and weather-blanched the board— however ancient the building itself—in its business there are no indications of decay, and it still does a thriving trade. Guests of the excursionist kind occasionally dine there; while in the angling season, *piscator* stays at it all through spring and summer; and if a keen disciple of Izaak, or an ardent

admirer of the Wye scenery, often prolong-
ing his sojourn into late autumn. Besides,
from towns not too distant, the sporting
tradesmen and fast clerks, after early closing
on Saturdays, come hither, and remain over
till Monday, for the first train catchable at
a station some two miles off.

The "Welsh Harp" can provide beds for
all, and sitting rooms besides. For it is a
roomy *caravanserai*, and if a little rough in
its culinary arrangements, has a cellar unex-
ceptionable. Among those who taste its
tap are many who know good wine from
bad, with others who only judge of the
quality by the price; and in accordance
with this criterion the Boniface of the
" Harp "? can give them the very best.

It is a Saturday night, and two of those
last described connoisseurs, lately arrived at
the Wyeside hostelry, are standing before
its bar counter, drinking rhubarb sap, which
they facetiously call "fizz," and believe to
be champagne. As it costs them ten shillings the bottle they are justified in their
belief; and quite as well will it serve their

purpose. They are young drapers' assist-
ants from a large manufacturing town, out
for their hebdomadal holiday, which they
have elected to spend in an excursion to the
Wye, and a frolic at Rugg's Ferry.

They have had an afternoon's boating on
the river ; and, now returned to the " Harp "
—their place of put-up—are flush of talk
over their adventures, quaffing the sham
" shammy," and smoking " regalias," not
anything more genuine.

While thus indulging they are startled
by the apparition of what seems an angel,
but what they know to be a thing of flesh
and blood—something that pleases them
better—a beautiful woman. More correctly
speaking a girl ; since it is Mary Morgan
who has stepped inside the room set apart
for the distributing of drink.

Taking the cigars from between their
teeth—and leaving the rhubarb juice, just
poured into their glasses, to discharge its
pent-up gas—they stand staring at the girl,
with an impertinence rather due to the drink
than any innate rudeness. They are harm-

less fellows in their way; would be quiet enough behind their own counters; though fast before that of the "Welsh Harp," and foolish with such a face as that of Mary Morgan beside them.

She gives them scant time to gaze on it. Her business is simple, and speedily transacted.

"A bottle of your best brandy — the French cognac?" As she makes the demand, placing ten shillings, the price understood, upon the lead-covered counter.

The barmaid, a practised hand, quickly takes the article called for from a shelf behind, and passes it across the counter, and with like alertness counting the shillings laid upon it, and sweeping them into the till.

It is all over in a few seconds' time; and with equal celerity Mary Morgan, slipping the purchased commodity into her cloak, glides out of the room—vision-like as she entered it.

"Who is that young lady?" asks one of the champagne drinkers, interrogating the barmaid.

"Young lady!" tartly returns the latter, with a flourish of her heavily chignoned head, "only a farmer's daughter."

"Aw!" exclaims the second tippler, in drawling imitation of Swelldom, "only the offspring of a chaw-bacon! she's a monstrously crummy creetya, anyhow."

"Devilish nice gal!" affirms the other, no longer addressing himself to the barmaid, who has scornfully shown them the back of her head, with its tower of twisted jute. "Devilish nice gal, indeed! Never saw spicier stand before a counter. What a dainty little fish for a farmer's daughter! Say, Charley! wouldn't you like to be sellin' her a pair of kids—Jouvin's best—helpin' her draw them on, eh?"

"By Jove, yes! That would I."

"Perhaps you'd prefer it being boots? What a stepper she is, too! S'pose we slide after, and see where she hangs out?"

"Capital idea! Suppose we do?"

"All right, old fellow! I'm ready with the yard stick—roll off!"

And without further exchange of their

professional phraseology, they rush out, leaving their glasses half full of the effervescing beverage—rapidly on the spoil.

They have sallied forth to meet disappointment. The night is black as Erebus, and the girl gone out of sight. Nor can they tell which way she has taken; and to inquire might get them "guyed," if not worse. Besides, they see no one of whom inquiry could be made. A dark shadow passes them, apparently the figure of a man; but so dimly descried, and going in such rapid gait, they refrain from hailing him.

Not likely they will see more of the "monstrously crummy creetya" that night—they may on the morrow somewhere—perhaps at the little chapel close by.

Registering a mental vow to do their devotions there, and recalling the bottle of fizz left uncorked on the counter they return to finish it.

And they drain it dry, gulping down several goes of B.-and-S., besides, ere ceasing to think of the "devilish nice gal," on whose dainty little fist they would so like fitting kid gloves.

Meanwhile, she, who has so much interested the dry goods gentlemen, is making her way along the road which leads past the Widow Wingate's cottage, going at a rapid pace, but not continuously. At intervals she makes stops, and stands listening—her glances sent interrogatively to the front. She acts as one expecting to hear footsteps, or a voice in friendly salutation—and see him saluting, for it is a man.

Footsteps are there besides her own, but not heard by her, nor in the direction she is hoping to hear them. Instead, they are behind, and light, though made by a heavy man. For he is treading gingerly as if on eggs—evidently desirous not to make known his proximity. Near he is, and were the light only a little clearer she would surely see him. Favoured by its darkness he can follow close, aided also by the shadowing trees, and still further from her attention being all given to the ground in advance, with thoughts pre-occupied.

But closely he follows her, but never coming up. When she stops he does the same, moving on again as she moves forward. And so for several pauses, with spells of brisk walking between.

Opposite the Wingates' cottage she tarries longer than elsewhere. There was a woman standing in the door, who, however, does not observe her—cannot—a hedge of holly between. Cautiously parting its spinous leaves and peering through, the young girl takes a survey, not of the woman, whom she well knows, but of a window—the only one in which there is a light. And less the window than the walls inside. On her way to the Ferry she had stopped to do the same; then seeing shadows—two of them—one a woman's, the other of a man. The woman is there in the door—Mrs. Wingate herself; the man, her son, must be elsewhere.

"Under the elm, by this," says Mary Morgan, in soliloquy. "I'll find him there"—she adds, silently gliding past the gate.

"Under the elm," mutters the man who

follows, adding, "I'll kill her there—ay, both!"

Two hundred yards further on, and she reaches the place where the footpath debouches upon the road. There is a stile of the usual rough crossbar pattern, proclaiming a right of way.

She stops only to see there is no one sitting upon it—for there might have been—then leaping lightly over, she proceeds along the path.

The shadow behind does the same, as though it were a spectre pursuing.

And now, in the deeper darkness of the narrow way, arcaded over by a thick canopy of leaves, he goes closer and closer, almost to touching. Were a light at this moment let upon his face, it would reveal features set in an expression worthy of hell itself; and cast farther down, would show a hand closed upon the haft of a long-bladed knife —nervously clutching—every now and then half drawing it from its sheath, as if to plunge its blade into the back of her who is now scarce six steps ahead!

And with this dread danger threatening
—so close—Mary Morgan proceeds along
the forest path, unsuspectingly : joyfully,
as she thinks of who is before, with no
thought of that behind—no one to cry out,
or even whisper, the word : " Beware ! "

CHAPTER XX.

IN more ways than one has Jack Wingate thrown dust in his mother's eyes. His going to the Ferry after a piece of whipcord and a bit of pitch was fib the first; the second his not going there at all—for he has not. Instead, in the very opposite direction; soon as reaching the road, having turned his face towards Abergann, though his objective point is but the "big elm." Once outside the gate he glides along the holly hedge crouchingly, and with head ducked, so that it may not be seen by the good dame, who has followed him to the door.

The darkness favouring him, it is not; and congratulating himself at getting off thus deftly, he continues rapidly up the road.

Arrived at the stile, he makes stop, saying in soliloquy :—

" I take it she be sure to come ; but I'd gi'e something to know which o' the two ways. Bein' so darkish, an' that plank a bit dangerous to cross, I ha' heard—'tan't often I cross it—just possible she may choose the roundabout o' the road. Still, she sayed the big elm, an' to get there she'll have to take the path comin' or goin' back. If I thought comin' I'd steer straight there an' meet her. But s'posin' she prefers the road, that 'ud make it longer to wait. Wonder which it's to be."

With hand rested on the top rail of the stile, he stands considering. Since their stolen interchange of speech at the Harvest Home, Mary has managed to send him word she will make an errand to Rugg's Ferry ; hence his uncertainty. Soon again he resumes his conjectured soliloquy :—

" 'Tan't possible she ha' been to the Ferry, an' goed back again ? God help me, I hope not ! An' yet there's just a chance.

I weesh the Captain hadn't kep' me so long down there. An' the fresh from the rain that delayed us nigh half a hour, I oughtn't to a stayed a minute after gettin' home. But mother cookin' that nice bit o' steak; if I hadn't ate it she'd a been angry, and for certain suspected somethin'. Then listenin' to all that dismal stuff 'bout the corpse-candle. An' they believe it in the shire o' Pembroke! Rot the thing! Tho' I an't myself noways superstishus, it gi'ed me the creeps. Queer, her dreamin' she seed it go out o' Abergann! I do weesh she hadn't told me that; an' I mustn't say word o't to Mary. Tho' she ain't o' the fearsome kind, a thing like that's enough to frighten any one. Well, what'd I best do? If she ha' been to the Ferry an's goed home again, then I've missed her, and no mistake! Still, she said she'd be at the elim, an's never broke her promise to me when she cud keep it. A man ought to take a woman at her word—a true woman—an' not be too quick to antici- pate. Besides, the surer way's the safer.

She appointed the old place, an' there I'll abide her. But what am I thinkin' o'? She may be there now, a waitin' for me!"

He doesn't stay by the stile one instant longer, but, vaulting over it, strikes off along the path.

Despite the obscurity of the night, the narrowness of the track, and the branches obstructing, he proceeds with celerity. With that part he is familiar—knows every inch of it, well as the way from his door to the place where he docks his boat—at least so far as the big elm, under whose spreading branches he and she have oft clandestinely met. It is an ancient patriarch of the forest; its timber is honeycombed with decay, not having tempted the axe by whose stroke its fellows have long ago fallen, and it now stands amid their progeny, towering over all. It is a few paces distant from the footpath, screened from it by a thicket of hollies interposed between, and extending around. From its huge hollow trunk a buttress, horizontally projected, affords a convenient seat for two, making it the very *beau ideal* of a trysting-tree.

Having got up and under it, Jack Wingate is a little disappointed—almost vexed —at not finding his sweetheart there. He calls her name—in the hope she may be among the hollies—at first cautiously and in a low voice, then louder. No reply; she has either not been, or has and is gone.

As the latter appears probable enough, he once more blames Captain Ryecroft, the rain, the river flood, the beefsteak—above all, that long yarn about the *canwyll corph*, muttering anathemas against the ghostly superstition.

Still she may come yet. It may be but the darkness that's delaying her. Besides, she is not likely to have the fixing of her time. She said she would " find a way ; " and having the will—as he believes—he flatters himself she will find it, despite all obstructions.

With confidence thus restored, he ceases to pace about impatiently, as he has been doing ever since his arrival at the tree; and, taking a seat on the buttress, sits listening with all ears. His eyes are of little use in the Cimmerian gloom. He can barely make out the forms of the holly bushes, though they are almost within reach of his hand.

But his ears are reliable, sharpened by love; and, ere long they convey a sound, to him sweeter than any other ever heard in that wood—even the songs of its birds. It is a swishing, as of leaves softly brushed by the skirts of a woman's dress—which it is. He needs no telling who comes. A subtle electricity, seeming to precede, warns him of Mary Morgan's presence, as though she were already by his side.

All doubts and conjectures at an end, he starts to his feet, and steps out to meet her. Soon as on the path he sees a cloaked figure, drawing nigh with a grace of movement distinguishable even in the dim glimmering light.

"That you, Mary?"

A question mechanical; no answer expected or waited for. Before any could be given she is in his arms, her lips hindered from words by a shower of kisses.

Thus having saluted, he takes her hand and leads her among the hollies. Not from precaution, or fear of being intruded upon. Few besides the farm people of Abergann use the right-of-way path, and unlikely any of them being on it at that hour. It is only from habit they retire to the more secluded spot under the elm, hallowed to them by many a sweet remembrance.

They sit down side by side; and close, for his arm is around her waist. How unlike the lovers in the painted pavilion at Llangorren! Here there is neither concealment of thought nor restraint of speech —no time given to circumlocution—none wasted in silence. There is none to spare, as she has told him at the moment of meeting.

"It's kind o' you comin', Mary," he says, as soon as they are seated. "I knew ye would."

"O Jack! What a work I had to get out—the trick I've played mother! You'll laugh when you hear it."

"Let's hear it, darling!"

She relates the catastrophe of the cupboard, at which he does laugh beyond measure, and with a sense of gratification. Six shillings thrown away—spilled upon the floor—and all for him! Where is the man who would not feel flattered, gratified, to be the shrine of such sacrifice, and from such a worshipper?

"You've been to the Ferry, then?"

"You see," she says, holding up the bottle.

"I weesh I'd known that. I could a met ye on the road, and we'd had more time to be thegither. It's too bad, you havin' to go straight back."

"It is. But there's no help for it. Father Rogier will be there before this, and mother mad impatient."

Were in light she would see his brow darken at mention of the priest's name. She does not, nor does he give expression

to the thoughts it has called up. In his
heart he curses the Jesuit—often has with
his tongue, but not now. He is too
delicate to outrage her religious suscepti-
bilities. Still he cannot be altogether
silent on a theme so much concerning
both.

"Mary dear!" he rejoins in grave, serious
tone, "I don't want to say a word against
Father Rogier, seein' how much he be your
mother's friend; or, to speak more truthful,
her favourite; for I don't believe he's
the friend o' anybody. Sartinly, not
mine, nor yours; and I've got it on my
mind that man will some day make mischief
between us."

"How can he, Jack?"

"Ah, how! A many ways. One, his
sayin' ugly things about me to your mother
—tellin' her tales that ain't true."

"Let him—as many as he likes; you
don't suppose I'll believe them?"

"No, I don't, darling—'deed I don't."

A snatched kiss affirms the sincerity of
his words; hers as well, in her lips not

being drawn back, but meeting him half-way.

For a short time there is silence. With that sweet exchange thrilling their hearts it is natural.

He is the first to resume speech; and from a thought the kiss has suggested:—

"I know there be a good many who'd give their lives to get the like o' that from your lips, Mary. A soft word, or only a smile. I've heerd talk o' several. But one's spoke of, in particular, as bein' special favourite by your mother, and backed up by the French priest."

"Who?"

She has an idea who—indeed knows; and the question is only asked to give opportunity of denial.

"I dislike mentionin' his name. To me it seems like insultin' ye. The very idea o' Dick Dempsey——"

"You needn't say more," she exclaims, interrupting him. "I know what you mean. But you surely don't suppose I could think of him as a sweetheart? That *would* insult me."

"I hope it would; pleezed to hear you say't. For all, he thinks o' you, Mary; not only in the way o' sweetheart, but——"

He hesitates.

"What?"

"I won't say the word. 'Tain't fit to be spoke—about him an' you."

"If you mean *wife*—as I suppose you do—listen! Rather than have Richard Dempsey for a husband, I'd die—go down to the river and drown myself! That horrid wretch! I hate him!"

"I'm glad to hear you talk that way—right glad."

"But why, Jack? You know it couldn't be otherwise! You should—after all that's passed. Heaven be my witness! you I love, and you alone. You only shall ever call me wife. If not—then nobody!"

"God bless ye!" he exclaims in answer to her impassioned speech. "God bless you, darling!" in the fervour of his gratitude flinging his arms around, drawing her to his bosom, and showering upon her lips an avalanche of kisses.

With thoughts absorbed [in the delirium of love, their souls for a time surrendered to it, they hear not a rustling among the late fallen leaves; or, if hearing, supposed it to proceed from bird or beast—the flight of an owl, with wings touching the twigs; or a fox quartering the cover in search of prey. Still less do they see a form skulking among the hollies, black and boding as their shadows.

Yet such there is; the figure of a man, but with face more like that of demon—for it is he whose name has just been upon their lips. He has overheard all they have said; every word an added torture, every phrase sending hell to his heart. And now, with jealousy in its last dire throe, every remnant of hope extinguished — cruelly crushed out—he stands, after all, unresolved how to act. Trembling, too; for he is at bottom a coward. He might rush at them and kill both—cut them to pieces with the knife he is holding in his hand. But if only one, and that her, what of himself! He has an instinctive fear of Jack Wingate,

who has more than once taught him a sub-
duing lesson.

That experience stands the young waterman in stead now, in all likelihood saving
his life. For at this moment the moon,
rising, flings a faint light through the
branches of the trees; and like some
ravenous nocturnal prowler that dreads the
light of day, Richard Dempsey pushes his
knife-blade back into its sheath, slips out
from among the hollies, and altogether
away from the spot.

But not to go back to Rugg's Ferry, nor
to his own home. Well for Mary Morgan
if he had.

By the same glimpse of silvery light
warned as to the time, she knows she must
needs hasten away; as her lover, that he
can no longer detain her. The farewell kiss,
so sweet yet painful, but makes their parting more difficult; and, not till after repeating it over and over, do they tear
themselves asunder —he standing to look
after, she moving off along the woodland
path, as nymph or sylphide, with no

suspicion that a satyr has preceded her and is waiting not far 'off, with foul fell intent—no less than the taking of her life.

END OF VOL. I.

Woodfall & Kinder, Printers, Milford Lane, Strand, London, W.C.